The Canyon

Also by Stanley Crawford

FICTION

Gascoyne

Petroleum Man

Travel Notes

Log of the S.S. the Mrs. Unguentine

Some Instructions to My Wife Concerning the Upkeep of the House and Marriage, and to My Son and Daughter Concerning the Conduct of Their Childhood

Seed

NONFICTION

Mayordomo: Chronicle of an Acequia in Northern New Mexico

A Garlic Testament: Seasons on a Small New Mexico Farm

The River in Winter: New and Selected Essays

The Canyon

a novel

Stanley Crawford

UNIVERSITY OF NEW MEXICO PRESS ❧ ALBUQUERQUE

Library of Congress Cataloging-in-Publication Data
Crawford, Stanley G., 1937–
    The canyon : a novel / Stanley Crawford.
       pages ; cm
    ISBN 978-0-8263-5561-4 (softcover : acid-free paper) —
    ISBN 978-0-8263-5562-1 (ebook)
    1. Nineteen fifties—Fiction I. Title.
    PS3553.R295C36 2015
    813'.54—dc23
                                            2014019826

Cover illustration courtesy of Christina Frain
Cover designed by Lila Sanchez
Typeset by Felicia Cedillos
Composed in Sabon 10.5/15
Display fonts are Maximus LT Std and Callie Hand

For Mark Sainsbury and Victoria Goodman

One

I WAS HUNKERED down into a ball listening in the shadows as they sat on the couch and armchairs grouped around the massive stone fireplace, where a fire flickered, about to go out. Dad stood, tipped back the fire screen, threw the end of his cigarette on the coals, then piled on some bits of bark for kindling and a couple of piñon logs. The group of four watched them smolder. When the fire *poof*ed back into flame, they resumed murmuring to each other between sips of the cough medicine–like brandy.

Scotty, what are you going to do with this place? asked my aunt, Dad's sister, in her high yet throaty voice, with a sudden loudness, as if to announce it was time to get serious about something. Her fixed stare at some article of dress of mine or tufts of hair that always stood up on the back of my head or my dirty fingernails would cause me to stand stock-still until her attention wandered off to something more interesting or urgent, and she would proclaim, often to no one in particular, Those picture frames simply must be dusted. If there's anything I can't stand, it's dusty picture frames.

I've approached the Forest Service, Dad said. He was crouched before the fireplace, back turned to the others, poking again at the reluctant fire. An afternoon thunderstorm had cooled the air. This was our first fire of late summer.

You'd certainly be relieved, wouldn't you, Irma?

I beg your pardon, said Mother in an absent voice that suggested she hadn't been listening. I think I have a migraine coming on.

Whatever a migraine was I knew its "coming on" was a signal that she would soon get up and excuse herself to climb up the stairs and close the door to her room. On the way she'd probably see me crouching under the stairs. It was unpredictable whether she'd ignore me or make a fuss over my being there and therefore draw the attention of the others. I didn't want to go back to my room. Mickey was in a roughhousing mood. I just wanted to crouch or lie here listening to the adults natter away the evening against the low hiss of the fire.

Mother got up, took her glass to the kitchen, and approached the staircase at an angle from which I was not visible. Her footsteps clomped loudly up over my head and then echoed down the long hall to her room at the end; the thumb latch rattled open and closed. After a while some water ran.

Aunt Ruby's back was to me. To her left was an old lamp made out of a shotgun once owned by Dad's father, with a riveted copper shade dark with tarnish. With Mother gone, Ruby sprawled out on the sofa and twisted a cigarette into a short ivory holder. Her brown hair was coifed into a scalloped shape;

she always made it clear at the beginning that her stays at the lodge were limited by the date of her next appointment with her Denver hairdresser, usually in a week or less.

What would Father think, Scotty? I think it was Aunt Clara who told me that the fireplace was built by our grandfather with his own hands.

Dad got to his feet and turned in her direction. When others stood he was often the shortest in the room. His shiny bald pate was an object of fascination for the occasional friend of mine who made it up to the lodge. Behind him the dark basalt walls and high ceiling of fat beams blackened over the years by wood smoke were barely visible in the gloom.

Aunt Ruby's husband, Walter, stood up from a wobbly arm-chair made of small logs whose smooth bark had shrunk under the varnish like wrinkled skin. More brandy, anyone?

In the kitchen, on the table, Dad suggested.

Walter was tall and thin, and dressed in shiny dark suits that were out of place at the lodge. He and Aunt Ruby had arrived the day before in a new maroon Mercury with the top down, looking flushed and grimy from the last seventeen miles of rough winding dirt road and the radiator boiling over. Dad had told Walter to keep the engine running while he dribbled cold water over the radiator from a huge aluminum teakettle.

I probably couldn't sell it, in the end, Dad said into the fire.

Of course not, Ruby shot back. Scotty Junior will want it, won't he?

It had never occurred to me that the lodge might someday be mine. I didn't yet know what happened when people died because they had only done so a very long time ago in faraway places, even Ruby's first husband, about the time I was born.

Though you know, of course, Ruby continued after a long pause, that if or when the mine goes you'll have much less reason to come up here.

When, I would think.

Now wouldn't that be a relief?

They momentarily locked eyes. A door clattered open upstairs, my own, and footsteps shuffled down the hall and skipped down the stairs over my head, then stopped just before the last step. Mickey leaned way over the fat log that made up the banister and whispered down at me too loudly, What are you doing there?

Ruby and Walter, who had returned with fuller snifters of brandy, turned in our direction.

You boys should have been in bed a long time ago, she said.

Mickey was Ruby's son but not Walter's. They had come to take him back to Denver, where they spent their summers, after Mickey's month's stay with us to give me some company, which I alternately welcomed and resented. When we weren't fighting, he was my cousin. When we were, he was a "half cousin." At the moment I was more interested in Aunt Ruby and Walter, whom I watched and spied on, seeking to learn the secrets of what made them so exotic compared to my ordinary parents, who always seemed sunk in the agonies of living from day to day. Whenever Aunt Ruby arrived she turned the huge pile of dark rocks and heavy beams and wavy, creaking plank floors that made up the lodge into a palace of imperfect wonders within which we were all lucky to be living.

Mickey and I shuffled upstairs to my room. I didn't tell him he made us miss out on a chance to sip some of the brandy from the half-empty glasses the adults would sometimes leave behind when they went to bed. He already had his pajamas on. I followed him down the hall to my room and shut the door behind us. The upper bunk was littered with comic books Mickey had read through again and again. I still had not succeeded in finding the stubby little cartoon book of dirty pictures he'd stolen from his stepfather's drawer, which he thumbed through pressed up against the wall in bed, his back to the room, and never let me see. He climbed up on the bunk and assumed his furtive reading position.

Let me have a look.

No.

I sat down on the lower bunk and pulled off my clothes and put on my pajama bottoms. Chilly downstairs on late-summer evenings, the lodge was always stuffy upstairs until about midnight, even with the window propped open with a stick and the hallway French doors wide open, admitting the low hiss of the river and occasional muted bangs and crackling sounds from up in the canyon, and choruses of coyotes in the early evening and at dawn and during full moons. The upstairs bedrooms with walls of darkened tongue-and-groove pine were arranged in two rows like a dormitory, though the three across the hall now served only for storage. My bedroom was next to the guest bedroom, in turn next to my parents' bedroom, the largest of the three and the only one with its own bathroom and with windows on two sides, which gave it the best ventilation.

I turned out the light.

Hey, I'm not ready.

Let me have a look then.

No.

I expected Mickey to climb down and turn the light back

on. He might leave the little book lying on his pillow. I would lunge. But we were both distracted by the sound of footsteps out in the hall and then the clattering of Aunt Ruby and Walter's door opening and closing. The light stayed off. Whenever Aunt Ruby was walking around downstairs I tried to position myself behind her in order to glimpse the dark straight seam of her nylon stockings down the back of her full voluptuous calves, which I found much less fascinating when fully bared down at the river. Of the various women I knew, teachers and mothers of friends, Aunt Ruby's calves were much the best, and she wore a somewhat darker shade of nylons than most, which also seemed exotic and daring. Whenever she was at the lodge freshly washed nylons waved in the breeze on the line next to the outhouse out back, and I kept track of their comings and goings to make certain that the system of keeping Aunt Ruby's legs sheathed in nylons was working properly. After wartime shortages ended, she reveled in the new abundance, owned a dozen pair. Mother wore paler somewhat baggy stockings she didn't seem to care much about. Sometimes she rolled them over just above the knee, exposing a bulge of white flesh when she crossed her legs.

This was early for Aunt Ruby and Walter to come to bed. Sometimes the banging of the always-noisy door would wake me but I'd fall right back to sleep. Now I was still playing with images of how to sneak Mickey's book away from him and flip through the mysterious cartoon drawings. Absently I listened to the sounds next door through the thin wall. A squeal, a muffled crash, some faint laughing cries. Mickey was oddly still. There was none of the bouncing and squeaking by which he announced as often as he could that he was in the top bunk, me in the bottom. The sharp click of coat hangers against the wall, clothing or bedding sliding about. Then silence.

I went to sleep imagining her stockinged calves walking in high heels slowly up the stairs and down the hallway and back.

The next day at the lunch table Aunt Ruby fixed her eyes on Mickey as if becoming aware of his existence for the first time in hours. You should go have your last swim in the river. Take some soap.

Do we have to leave today?

She ignored him. Walter was asking Dad whether it was better to go up over the pass than to take the long way down through the canyon. Mickey had been trying to torment me with listing all the things he was going to do when he got back to Denver, but they paled compared to the luxury of having my own room to myself again for the three weeks left of our summer stay. And I knew my river was better than his backyard. Though I had to admit that the dime store he lived down the block from was a palace compared to the general store at Basalt Junction, fourteen miles downstream. I had steam engines puffing up and down the canyon twice a day. He had streetcars rumbling past their house every fifteen minutes. It mattered less that his corner house filled with family antiques was larger than ours on the other side of town, in a newer suburb.

Wait an hour before you go into the water, Aunt Ruby commanded as we got up from the table, this time fixing me with her stare. She was fond of describing the terrible paralytic cramps children would be seized with if they went into the water above their knees in less than an hour. Cheating by a minute could prove fatal. An hour, a full hour.

Mickey and I ran upstairs to change. This was complicated. He knew this could be an excuse for me to ransack the room in search of his cartoon book. We wouldn't change in the same room, each afraid that the other might *look*. He got inside the room first and slammed the door but missed latching it. We pushed back and forth against the flimsy boards. Heavy footsteps chugged up the stairs.

That's enough, boys, Walter grumbled before disappearing into the bathroom at the top of the stairs.

Mickey let the door open just long enough to toss out my swimming trunks, then slammed it closed and latched it. I had no choice but to slip into one of the unused rooms and change there. The one opposite my parents' was the least cluttered. I pushed the door open and entered the dim space filled with an old iron bedstead stacked high with gray mattresses, dining room chairs with ripped cane seats, empty gilt picture frames, an elk head missing an antler, a pile of bulging cardboard boxes whose contents I had not yet explored. A ripped yellow shade was pulled down over the closed window. I slipped off my jeans and undershorts. Adults had frequently made comments about how skinny or bony I was or about my posture, and I was shy about exposing my body. There was *naked* as part of doing something, taking a shower or a bath, drying myself with a towel, but I still knew nothing about being naked for the sake of it—other than when the daughter of recent houseguests and her two girlfriends had gone into the river with their bathing suits on and then had taken them off in the water and bounced up and down, flashing their small slippery breasts in the sun and then running out of the water and wrapping towels around themselves and letting them fall off and swathing themselves up again. I had watched from one of my hiding places in the rocks above the water. I wondered whether Mickey's picture book was like that. I stood naked in the semidarkness for a moment. Then I slipped on my satiny blue swimming trunks, feeling the embrace of the clammy material.

Hey, Scotty, where are you? Mickey called out from the hallway.

I kept silent. Walter emerged from the bathroom.

Did you see Scotty?

Probably waiting for you downstairs.

Walter's heavy footsteps descended the stairs. It sounded like Mickey went back into our room for a moment. I stood stock-still. Then he came back out and padded down the stairs in bare feet. Quietly I emerged, crossed the hallway, pushed open the door, climbed up on the upper bunk and searched under his pillow and blankets. I found nothing.

I caught sight of him a few minutes later at the far end of the sandy path that wandered down from the foot of the veranda through some cottonwoods to what everyone called "the beach," a crescent of fine gray sand on the outside of an S-bend in the river, where the water swirled slowly in circles before dropping into the low rapids of what gradually over the course of a half mile or so developed into the rough water of the Sluice Box. Upstream from the beach the water flowed at a leisurely pace around a bend through a relatively flat stretch, emerging from between piles of volcanic basalt boulders, out of which the two-story lodge had been built by Dad's grandfather. Whether he had performed this Herculean task with his own hands, as apparently he often boasted, or with the help of workers brought down from the silver mine, was a matter of family dispute.

Mickey turned around just as I emerged from the shadows. He was a shade darker than me, which I didn't know whether to connect to the dusky nylon stockings Aunt Ruby wore or to the fact that he was almost a year older than me, though we were in the same grade at school. Our instructions from the grown-ups were never to wade or paddle beyond a large black boulder that stuck up out of the water and marked the dividing line between the slow swirling water of the beach and the main flow of the river as it gathered speed and disappeared down below a mound of boulders and driftwood situated at the lower end of the beach, but in fact we often ventured out into the rapids, which were shallower than the adults remembered or imagined, where we lay back in the water and let it rush over our bodies. No one ever came down to check on us. A big bell on the veranda would summon us back for meals or as soon as the afternoon thunderheads began to gather, threatening downpours and flash floods.

When alone I was content to lie in the sand or poke through the driftwood or paddle out to the boulder and sit on its warm bulk, worn silky smooth by the water, and watch for trout darting from shadow to shadow, or scan the dark cliffsides for signs of a bald eagle, or run my eyes up and down the yellow gash of the railway line a hundred feet above the lodge to the east, wondering how long it would be before the afternoon train would puff and hiss and clank up the grade. With Mickey or other kids I always felt we had to do something. Now I only wished to be alone. A miasma of ill feeling had spread out between us. There were no more rocks left on the beach to try to make a dam with, and most of the driftwood of manageable size we had turned into boats to feed into the rapids, to see whose would win the race into foaming oblivion—to the annoyance of Dad, who saw perfectly good firewood thrown away.

I shuffled through the sand and sat on a huge brown stump half-buried in the sand. Mickey kicked at the water. He was wearing new maroon trunks, nearly the same color as the Mercury, with white string ties dangling down the front.

I'll show you the pictures, I thought I heard him say.

What?

I'll show you the pictures.

When?

When we go back inside. But you have to trade me something.

What?

You know.

There was only one thing I owned that Mickey coveted and that I kept hidden as cunningly as his picture book, and that was a cut-glass "ruby" the size of a small chicken egg. My grandfather had brought it back as a souvenir from the 1893 World's Fair in Chicago, and it had been given to me by Mother along with some other baubles when she was going through an old trunk years after his death. For a long time I thought Aunt Ruby was named after it. But Ruby wasn't her real name, I learned from her shortly before she died; she had so disliked her given name, Gertrude, that she renamed herself as soon as she left home, a daringly unheard-of act at the time. The family was scandalized: "Ruby" sounded lower class—or even vaguely ethnic as they might have said today.

I loved holding the cut-glass form up to the light and watching the kaleidoscopic images its finely cut bevels created, all bathed in deep scarlet. I knew it was the one object in the entire world that no one else but me possessed. Or more properly, that no one else I knew possessed anything remotely like it. Mickey had been scheming and bargaining for it ever since he began spending summers at the lodge with us, but until now he never had anything of comparable value.

Do I get to keep it? I asked after pondering the trade.

No, just to look at, he shot back.

Then I'll make you a deal, I called out. Mickey had moved away a few yards into the water. He was much more self-possessed in his body, which seemed more like an adult's, than I was with my gawky extremities, but I was sometimes quicker than he was.

I get to look at the pictures and you get to hold the ruby, and then we give them back to each other.

When?

When we're done looking.

No.

There the matter rested. I waded over to the boulder in the middle of the river and climbed up on it without taking a dip in the water. Mickey waded back to the beach and lay down on his stomach and began poking sticks and pine needles upright into the sand. Adults always fawned over him. How tall you're becoming. He's got his father's good looks. I'll bet you're strong. Except Aunt Ruby, who invariably scolded him. Mickey accepted both indifferently with a sniff and a twitch of his slightly pendulous lower lip, which he often strummed with his index finger, his blue-gray eyes staring fixedly in the distance.

Our sulking reveries were interrupted by the distant clang of the bell. Mickey stood up, brushed himself and strode off without waiting for me. I waded back across the water and followed him at a distance, watching him climb the flagstone steps of the veranda.

It hasn't been an hour, he called out to no one in particular.

Aunt Ruby's voice, sharper and higher pitched than usual, emerged from the open screen door. Come upstairs, young man, I want to talk to you.

The term *young man*, when used by either Aunt Ruby or Walter, always meant trouble. I followed him, but at the foot of the staircase up to the bedrooms I sensed that I shouldn't go up. Aunt Ruby and Walter were growling at each other, trying to stifle shouts. There was a slap, an *Ow!* from Mickey.

Where do you get such trash? Aunt Ruby shrieked. A few minutes later Mickey, fully dressed now but still in bare feet, ran down the stairs clutching his small suitcase. Upstairs, Walter's low plaintive voice suggested attempts at an excuse. Mickey stopped and looked past me into space for an instant. Phew, he said with the quick little smile of someone who is often caught in the act, before walking on through the living room and dining room and kitchen and out to the back, where the Mercury convertible was waiting, its hood and trunk both up, its top down. I followed on his heels, thinking it was safer to be outside. Dad was leaning inside the engine compartment, replacing the dipstick. Walter was helpless at such things. As Mickey climbed into the backseat, he turned to me and whispered, She found it.

A moment later Walter emerged from the back door dressed in shirt and tie and suspenders and carrying two suitcases. He was flushed and sweating. After lifting the suitcases into the trunk, he tried to look around and pretend that nothing was the matter, thanked Dad, patted him on the back.

Sorry she's not feeling too good, he said, but tell Irma what a good time we had, and . . .

He stopped short. Aunt Ruby closed the back door behind her and walked around the car and with a flash of nylon-clad calves climbed into the passenger side and slammed the door. She was made up in a way that suggested that a luncheon date was half a block away, not seventeen miles on a dirt road and another hundred on the highway. A glossy black hat with a wisp of a veil was pinned to her hair. She twisted around and held my eye with her stare. Even though I hadn't seen the pictures, I knew I was guilty. I had wanted to. My face reddened. I broke into a sweat. She turned away.

Walter climbed in behind the wheel and slammed the door. But even this he didn't do quite right. Dad grabbed the handle and pulled the door open and slammed it shut again, hard enough this time that it latched. Walter started the engine, put it into gear, drove off with an awkward wave. Mickey's head slowly disappeared as he slouched even deeper into the backseat. Aunt Ruby stared straight ahead.

That afternoon I discovered Mickey's shoes and socks under the bed, too late for them to think of turning around and coming back.

Two

WITH MICKEY GONE I was free to long for the arrival of Rosalind, whose exotic name excited me almost as much as her physical presence. I regretted not having the pictures, with which to bargain with her for some undefined trade or favor, though from Aunt Ruby's simmering outrage I also sensed some deep inappropriateness in the thought.

Dad assumed that Rosalind and her parents and little brother would arrive in a few days' time but the expected telegram had not yet shown up. Every morning, as soon as he heard the throaty puffing of the northbound train a half mile down the tracks, he would climb up through the boulders to the narrow-gauge rail line and wait for the train to round the bend. It ascended the steep grade at little more than a walking pace. At the sight of Dad, the engineer would give a short hoot with his whistle to alert the conductor, who would then lean out the open door of the combination baggage and passenger car to see whether Dad was standing with a suitcase in hand and would therefore need help climbing up on to the steps of the moving train, or whether he was just waiting for the mail and the occasional telegram. The engineer would wave as he chugged past, and then the conductor, Mr. Sanchez, would climb down to the lower step and reach out and hand the mail to Dad. Sometimes he would even step down and stand and chat for a moment until the second and last passenger car rolled by, grabbing the last curved handrail and swinging himself back on board.

Nothing today, Mr. Alton, had been the response for several afternoons.

When Dad was up at the mine, I did this duty even though Mother scolded me for coming back with soot spots on my clothes, and I often went up with Dad just to watch the steam engine chewing and clanking its way up the grade. The sound of the morning train was a signal for Mother to pull any washing off the clothesline she might have left out overnight. Later in the afternoons I would go down to the river to savor being alone again and lay in the sand and let Rosalind's name roll around in my head and linger on my tongue. I knew her from two previous brief summertime visits to the lodge but would have been hard-pressed to describe her in any way, other than that she was *Rosalind*. It seemed of little importance that she was nearsighted and walked around in a haze unmindful of those around her, with the same abstracted look that Mickey sometimes assumed, or that she had become a reader of unbreakable concentration once she picked up a book, or that her legs were long and skinny, but it was just these aspects that I fixated on when I thought of her. I could count on one hand the moments she seemed to focus on my presence during the long hours and days we had spent together at the lodge, mostly in silence, on the edge of our parents' games of cards in the evening, our fathers' rare times of fishing in the river, hikes down to the Sluice Box, and a single drive down and back to Basalt Junction in the family cars. These centered around a wisecrack of mine, a foolhardy stunt with the swing-sofa on the veranda, and a few other displays of daring, but when in a moment of overconfidence last summer I had slowly uncapped my hands to reveal the deep-red ruby, she only squinted at it briefly before looking up at me quizzically as if to say, So what? She had been sitting on the sofa in front of the fireplace about to pick up her book. With that absence that I so longed to break through and be encompassed within, she finally asked, Is that from your father's mine? I slipped the egg-sized piece of glass back into my pocket and turned away, trying to think of other ways to attract her attention.

Mr. and Mrs. Slatter were a cheerful and good-natured couple, unlike most of my moody severe relatives, tall and fair-haired, *strapping*, as Aunt Ruby had once called them, *a strapping couple*, with a touch of scorn in her voice. I didn't know what *strapping* meant but my eyes were drawn to Mrs. Slatter's broad strong calves, whose flawless tan made it hard to see when she was wearing nylons, at least from the front. I couldn't keep my eyes off them unless to look at her smooth tanned arms. She wore sunglasses with small green lenses outdoors and sometimes even indoors, but she smiled so easily with her full somewhat pursed lips that no one complained. Mr. Slatter advised Dad on the geology of the mine; he had done his doctoral thesis, I was to understand much later, on a series of formations in the area. He had curly almost-blond hair, which Mrs. Slatter often reached over to tousle when they were sitting close to each other, which was much of the time. Mother and Dad rarely sat next to each other, except in the front seat of the LaSalle, and almost never touched, at least in my presence.

The Slatters didn't stay in the lodge, preferring instead to park their camping trailer just below the veranda and set up their two tents in the cottonwoods. On their first visit two years before, they had asked to camp on the beach but Dad said that sometimes during summer thunderstorms the water rose well up into the cottonwoods, even before the rains reached here, and it wouldn't be safe, particularly with the kids. Mr. and Mrs. Slatter slept in a large dark-green tent, and Rosalind and her six-year-old brother, Peter, in a brown pup tent. The warm, oily, waxy smell that emanated from the canvas in the heat of the afternoon was the exciting perfume of Rosalind's cocoon. She often read there as soon as the day warmed up, excluding Peter from the space.

Last summer I took to turning out my upstairs bedroom light at night and resting my chin on the sill of the open window, which looked down on their camp in front of the lodge, and watching the play of the flashlight beam inside Rosalind and Peter's tent, as they squirmed and yapped at each other. Usually the flashlight inside went on and off amid a chorus of little cries and the occasional bulge of something hitting the canvas.

Stop that.

Ouch.

Quit looking, will you?

I didn't say you could have that, give that back.

It's mine.

No it is not. Give it back.

I'll tell Mom.

These were typically more words than Rosalind had spoken to me in two days. After a while, the voices would stop and the beam would trace random patterns on the orange canvas, and finally the light would go out. A few minutes later, the shadowy figure of Mr. Slatter would step out of their tent and turn off the Coleman lantern on a folding table just outside the flap and go back inside.

On a night not long before the Slatters were supposed to leave that summer, a full moon was beginning to shine down into the canyon, its rays hitting the tops of the cottonwoods beyond the dark shapes of the tents. The river hissed. Far up the canyon some coyotes chattered. A dark shape, perhaps an owl, shot past the window and landed with a scrabbling sound somewhere up on the roof. Downstairs cool air would be flowing in through open windows and doors. I decided not to go to bed until the moonlight reached Rosalind's tent. Maybe she would emerge and I could signal her with my flashlight. But then what? I'll come downstairs and show you my . . . But if she thought nothing of my ruby, what would she like? Comic books? My collection of mineral chips labeled and glued to the bottom of a small cardboard box, a birthday gift from Dad three years ago? My well-worn *Aircraft Spotter's Guide* and a sheaf of pencil drawings of Luftwaffe Heinkels and Messerschmitts I had copied from its pages? I sat there at the window dreaming of her slipping out of her tent and padding up the stone steps into the lodge, in long soft flannel pajamas, and pushing open the door to my room. She would crouch down. What a lovely thing, she would say, lifting the ruby up and turning it around so its facets would catch the moonlight. (I dismissed niggling questions about why I had left it on the floor and how the moonlight would manage to enter my room when the moon was still in the eastern sky). Just as her mother had said earlier that day, carrying the gem out into the sunlight. What a lucky boy you are to have something like this. I'm sure you'll take good care of it the rest of your life, she had said, handing it back to me inside the veranda screen door.

I got up and pulled off my clothes and slipped into my pajamas in the semidarkness and then went back to the window. I was about to close it partway when something moved in front of Mr. and Mrs. Slatter's tent. The moon had crested the wall of the canyon and the roof of the lodge, illuminating the scene below. It was Mr. Slatter, who stepped out in front of the tent and glanced up at the lodge and then tiptoed barefoot over to a clump of grass. He was stark-naked. His back to me, his untanned buttocks glowing in the moonlight as huge as a horse's, it seemed, he peed into the grass, shook his penis vigorously, and then tiptoed back toward the tent, the long thing wagging back and forth. I had never seen a naked adult before or certainly could not remember seeing one, though Mickey said he was always coming on Aunt Ruby with nothing on, darting between her bedroom and the bathroom. Mr. Slatter slipped inside the tent. A moment later Mrs. Slatter emerged, also naked. I held my breath at the sight of her full white breasts. She followed in his footsteps and squatted not far from where he had peed but for a much longer time, head lowered. I could almost not bear to look. I was seized with uncontrollable shivering. Then she stood up and walked daintily back to the tent, feet arched to avoid stickers. I wondered what might be inside the muff of dark hair between her ample thighs.

Next morning honking up at the lodge scattered these reveries. I had just come down to the beach. I stood up and brushed the sand from my swimming trunks and patted down an uncomfortable swelling. Through the trees I could make out the Slatters' two-tone gray Studebaker sedan and the flat wooden camping trailer behind with its orange-brown canvas cover. From a rear door Rosalind's legs emerged. She had on long red socks.

Embarrassed to be seen in my trunks, I ran up through the edge of the cottonwoods and around to the back door of the lodge and in through the kitchen, the odor of burning pine emanating from the range, and up the stairs to my room, where I changed. When I came down the Slatters and Mother and Dad were chatting on the veranda.

Where's Rosalind? I asked with feigned casualness.

Mrs. Slatter turned and held out a hand. How you have grown, she said with a warm smile. You're going to be the tallest of them all.

Finding clothes for him . . . Mother began.

He's bound to stop one of these days. Rosalind has begun to fill out a little, at least. I don't remember so many beanpoles around when I was their age. Mrs. Slatter turned back to me. She can't wait to see you again, Scotty.

But where was she? Below, the Studebaker doors were open

and no one was inside. I felt it would be impolite to repeat my too-brusque question. Mrs. Slatter turned back to Mother, who was holding a fixed tight little smile in her direction, trying to look bright and enthusiastic, but I knew she was really wanting to find an excuse to disappear into her bedroom in order to adjust herself to the unexpectedly early arrival of houseguests. Perhaps you should set up your tents, she finally blurted out, before it gets too hot. Or rains. Or something.

Mrs. Slatter took this in with a slightly uncertain glance, then resumed what must have been an earlier conversation: I had forgotten you had a library here, Irma. How fortunate. We were fifty miles out of Denver when Rosalind told Harold to stop the car, she had forgotten her box of books, everything except what she was reading at that moment. Of course it was out of the question.

I slipped away. The library, so-called, was an alcove just beyond and beneath the staircase, its pine plank walls lined with sagging bookshelves. Before I was born or at least when I was very young Mother took to buying matched sets of the classics, a few of them bound in leather with gold lettering, and having them shipped up from Denver or out from Chicago. She hoped I would become the reader that she never quite managed to be. During our winters in town, Dad would take me to the public library once a week and guide me to bookshelves of stories about boys and dogs and horses, unmindful of the fact that my requests for a puppy were repeatedly evaded because we moved around too much to keep pets. I would dutifully check a few books out each week and pretend to read through them. I knew quite enough about dogs through friends and didn't like horses, and the boys of the stories seemed to have only grand moral dilemmas and none of the agonizing little problems that could make my life miserable—like erections most recently, a word not yet in my vocabulary. Was I the only one this happened to? I was becoming obsessed at hairs sprouting on somewhat older boys' faces and wondered about the exact moment or hour or day they had begun shaving, which I imagined to be a deeply troubling business, especially having to go into a drugstore somewhere and actually buy the razor, under the smirking eyes of adults. At any rate I was much more curious about all the other shelves in the public library, which Dad thought inappropriate or too grown-up for me, while Mother's exceptions about our own little library room overwhelmed me from the opposite direction. A few weeks before leaving Denver, they did buy me a set of illustrated encyclopedias, half of which I went through page by page, with unbounded fascination. But Dad wouldn't have them shipped up to the lodge.

Rosalind was standing in the gloomy little room staring at the shelf in front of her. I paused at the low doorway, wondering if anyone had cleaned up the mouse turds deposited on the shelves during our winter absences. My heart was pounding. She reached up and pulled out the fattest volume on the shelf and tucked it under her arm. Finally she twisted around in my direction. She had on her black-rimmed glasses that turned up at the corners.

I forgot my book box.

I know.

Most of the ones I was going to read are here.

They are?

I hate summer vacation.

She slipped past me and headed across the living room

toward the veranda, where the adults were still talking. I stared at the rows and rows of books. Some of the volumes from matched sets had been misshelved or were missing. Mice had chewed away at the pages' edges of many of the volumes, narrowing margins and scattering flakes of yellowed paper on the floor near the walls. Mother had lost interest in her project and rarely visited the alcove anymore, and Dad read mainly technical journals on mining and books on geology, which were mostly in cardboard boxes sticking out of the bottom shelves. The air smelled musty. At random I picked a book from the same shelf that Rosalind had taken hers from and carried it out into the living room, wondering where I could sit and read or pretend to read without attracting a flurry of comments from Mother or Dad or the Slatters, but where I might be visible to Rosalind, at least whenever she happened to look up from her book. This revealed itself to be an impossible condition. Since her tent was not yet set up, I suspected she was either hunched down in the veranda swing behind the adults or else in the backseat of the Studebaker.

I went back outside by way of the kitchen and back door and sauntered down past the eastern end of the veranda. She was in fact back inside the car, trying to push Peter out of the backseat. Feigning indifference, I walked closely past the front of the car, still warm from the recent drive, and then on down through the cottonwoods to the beach, where I climbed the highest boulder overlooking it and sat down, legs dangling over the edge, opened the book, and began to read, after verifying that she could probably see me from the backseat of the car. The book was *Jude the Obscure*, a title that promised lonely solidarity—at least as I look back on it now. I had no idea who

Thomas Hardy was. I had never pondered the relation of book to author. Books were books. The most useful book I had seen was an old hardback novel that Mickey had taken a hand drill and chisel to, hacking out most of the text to create a secret compartment for his firecrackers inside the closed covers. For the first few pages I kept glancing up in the direction of the Studebaker but soon I was drawn in by the words, the strange names, and the engulfing darkness of the scene, and was no longer thinking of Rosalind or playing with her name in my head.

I came back to myself when thunderheads cleared the high ridge above the canyon and blocked out the sun. The Studebaker had been moved to its habitual place, the camping trailer was unhitched, both tents were up, and Rosalind was nowhere in sight. Then from the depths of the canyon echoed the first faint chuffing sounds of the morning northbound train. Through the trees I caught sight of some movement up on the cliff: Dad and Mr. Slatter, small brown suitcases in hand, were picking their way up through boulders to the tracks. Below, Mother and Mrs. Slatter were pulling sheets and towels off the clothesline. Dad always took Mr. Slatter up to the mine for a day or two for advice on geology and engineering questions, about which they talked at great length before and after dinner out on the veranda, or next to the fireplace in the living room when it was cold and rainy. Mother discouraged such talk at the dinner table. From my rock I could see down the canyon where the engine was crawling around a bend above the Sluice Box and spewing black smoke from its stack, which spread out into a broad haze behind it. As it rounded the bend the black coal tender with a smear of once-white letters reading *DRG&W*

came into view, followed by a half dozen empty ore cars and ending with the rust-colored combination baggage and passenger car. Dad and Mr. Slatter had reached the rail line and had set down their suitcases and were looking upriver in the opposite direction.

The train wound slowly in and out of sight and then reached a short straight stretch where it always sounded very loud down at the lodge, a deep-throated puffing and a clanking of drive wheels and high-pitched squeals of dragging brake shoes and flanges of wheels scraping against the curved rails. Rosalind stepped out of her tent and looked up. From where she stood in front of the lodge, only the pulsations of black smoke shooting up into the air would be visible, and then the tops of the engine and taller cars as they rounded the bend directly above the lodge. A quick toot announced that the engineer had seen Dad and Mr. Slatter. The two returned his wave, picked up their suitcases. A minute later they tossed them into the open baggage-car door, where Mr. Sanchez, the conductor, slid them deeper inside, and then one by one they swung themselves up onto the steps of the rear platform. The sound of the engine would echo down the side of the canyon for almost another hour, rapidly fading after the locomotive crested the ridge, eight hundred feet above the river.

Rosalind had slipped back inside her tent. Peter was lying on his stomach on the ground outside doing something. I jumped down from the boulder and picked up a dried cottonwood leaf to mark my place. Never dog-ear the pages of a book, Aunt Ruby was fond of saying, as if that was an essential reading skill. Or a magazine. The clouds had retreated, perhaps only briefly, and the river was bright and clear and inviting again, and the water would be almost warm, but I didn't have my trunks on.

I decided to approach Rosalind in her forbidding pup tent. Peter, a cheerful little kid, was just that, a kid, and therefore not worthy of my attention, but he was lying next to the tent. I followed the path through the faintly rustling cottonwoods and reached the driveway in front of the lodge where the Slatters had set up camp. Precariously close to the tent fabric, Peter was burning holes in a piece of white cottonwood bark with a small magnifying glass, sending a thin plume of smoke skyward. He was slightly chubby with blond curly hair and the bright open face of both his mother and father, without Rosalind's angular look of being lost in thought. Whenever I approached, he looked at me expectantly, but I had nothing to offer except a cold *Hi* before going my way. Now, however, I wanted something.

Hi, Peter. Where's Rosalind?

I dunno.

You know perfectly well I'm in here, stupid, her voice came from inside the tent.

I was on the spot. I had asked where she was without thinking up a reason for wanting to see her. What could I make up? I was saved when Mrs. Slatter appeared on the front steps and called down, Where's Rosalind?

In her tent, Mrs. Slatter.

Peter, she scolded more sharply than I had ever heard her, please get up off the ground and brush yourself off right now.

She turned away and went back inside the lodge, perhaps having forgotten why she had been looking for Rosalind. I stood awkwardly a moment, expecting Rosalind to push aside the tent flap, but when she didn't I walked up the steps to the veranda and slouched down on the wicker swing-sofa, where I could see the top of her tent through the varnished log railing at the base of the rusty window screens. I rocked slowly back and forth, waiting. Inside the open screen door to the living room I could hear Mother and Mrs. Slatter now and then say a few words to each other between long pauses. They had never gotten on well, and these times alone together when the men were up at the mine were always tense.

Is he interested in girls yet? I could hear Mrs. Slatter asking cheerfully.

Mother took a moment to reply. Why, yes, there was someone in Chicago, I believe. Now what was her name? Another long pause. A Catholic girl. He wrote her letters.

My ears burned. I had no idea Mother knew about Annie.

How sweet. I'm worried about Rosalind's reading. It's all she's interested in.

A long silence. The tinkling of a spoon against a china teacup. Oh, it's a phase, Mother said wearily. I used to read so much when I was her age, and then—I stopped.

Oh?

I should put the roast in the oven. It will take forever.

Can I help?

The furniture creaked. No, thanks, I'm fine.

I could hear Mother walk into the kitchen and open the firebox to the wood range and shove in a couple of pieces of firewood. She banged shut the cast-iron door and slid open the draft control. Then the squeak of the oven door springs and some clattering noises as she transferred the roast from the sink counter to the oven. The door slammed shut. The Home Comfort range was of a hulking authority, with intricately scrolled nickel doors and panels. Guests, and especially children who were incredulous at how the massive appliance could have been moved to such a remote location, were sometimes teased by Aunt Ruby into believing that the range had been cast and forged on the spot and the lodge built around it—as I did for a long time, until my explorations behind it discovered an abundance of bolts and nuts and screws holding the thing together. Its fire burned and smoldered constantly through day and night. Mother hated it. I so miss my gas, she was fond of saying.

Mother stepped back into the living room and sat down.

When Harold gets back, Mrs. Slatter said, I hope we'll have some time again to hike up or down the canyon. Though I wouldn't be surprised if he wants to get going right away. We've been away for nearly five weeks.

Mother did not *hike* nor did any other of our family friends and relatives. The lodge was a place they visited in order to smoke and drink and sit and paddle in the river and admire the clouds. Occasionally the men would fish for trout for dinner. Now and then after dinner Mother would consent to walk up the driveway to the dirt road that ran along the tracks and amble along behind the smoking menfolk for a hundred yards or so, complaining about the gnats, the occasional mosquito, the possibilities of rattlesnakes, bats, skunks. Why does she even come here? I overheard Mrs. Slatter ask her husband during their last visit. Scotty, he replied, meaning my father, not me, because Scotty insists. He spent every summer of his childhood here.

There are so many rocks, Mother observed. You have to watch out for snakes.

In fact one afternoon while Dad was up at the mine—I was only two at the time—Mother bludgeoned to death with a dead cottonwood branch a six-foot-long diamondback she was convinced was going to slither up the stairs and inside; a photo in an album in the Denver house shows her holding with outstretched arms the dead creature by its rattles, leaning back as far away as she can from the dangling shape.

Mrs. Slatter didn't pursue the question of hikes. They fell into silence. I swung back and forth on the swing-sofa at a slow speed that triggered almost no creaking from the chains or the wicker frame. There was no sign of movement from Rosalind's tent. Peter had wandered off somewhere. The afternoon light was just beginning to soften. Swallows skimmed low between the cottonwoods and the lodge, suggesting the approach of a thunderstorm. I felt content swinging back and forth, listening to the mothers' desultory talk to my back and keeping an eye on Rosalind's tent at the foot of the wall below the veranda. With Dad and Mr. Slatter far away up on the mountainside, I was temporarily out of range of their unpredictable demands to somehow *grow up* through the completion of a new chore or task often involving knives or saws, shovels, hoes, hammers. Hiking seemed like one of those tasks that was supposed to help you grow up, but fortunately it was not on either Mother's or Dad's lists of requirements, which so far included keeping my room straightened, brushing my teeth and combing my hair, not doing certain things at the dining table, and speaking the formulas of courtesy at the right times. The problem was that none of these injunctions, even when followed assiduously, were connected with what being a grown-up seemed to be. Adults, perhaps excepting the Slatters, carried around within themselves something that was dark and brooding, which made it hard to pay attention to much outside of themselves. They lived their real lives out of sight, late at night or early in the morning, behind closed doors, or away from home, lives that seemed complex and unpredictable, perhaps even unknowable—at least compared to my little treasure box, which I considered the essence of who I was. It was where I hid my ruby—alternating with a knothole in the pine siding at the level of the pillow in the top bunk—a big silver Mexican coin Walter had once given me, and a few other baubles. But the adults probably knew about them, just as Mother had somehow found out about Annie and my two letters to her that she never responded to. They seemed to find out about everything, even Mickey's picture book.

Yet I had never made any sign of my obsession with Rosalind, so perhaps they didn't know about that. And as far as I could tell, nobody had caught me in the act of staring at Aunt Ruby's or Mrs. Slatter's strapping calves. The small round shiny scar on my left elbow where a cast from a broken arm had rubbed the skin raw when I was eight, that was a mark that no one else noticed anymore, even though I did, daily, or several times a day. These made up my collection of private little things inside some indefinable wall or fence that was in a sense parallel to my clothes but enclosed something else.

I had perfected a way of rocking back and forth on the swing-sofa in very short and precise tangents, silent except for random creakings of the wicker seat, body held rigid other than the propelling big toe, eyes fixed straight ahead. At the end of the forward swing I could make out the tip of the tent roof where it was held up by the front pole, the view of which then sank below the log railing as I retreated. Out of the corner of my eyes the details of the long porch were vague but present: the sagging tongue-and-groove ceiling painted a dirty cream, with mud dauber nests and daddy longlegs webs in the corners; the wicker armchairs with frayed armrests, and the peeling cream and light-green paint drawn up around a small wicker table on which sat a large dusty glass ashtray; the wavy plank floor; the dusty screens on the open sash windows that looked out across the veranda from the living room. A suggestion of a breeze wafted up a moldy odor from the crawl space beneath the lodge. I would have gone on forever swinging back and forth.

What are you reading?

The shadow to my left had startled me but the voice caused me to jump. I looked up. It was Mrs. Slatter. I had no idea what she was talking about. She pointed at the book lying on the cushion next to me. Afraid of trying to pronounce something in the title, I picked it up and handed it to her.

Oh, Rosalind has read that, too. What's it about?

I'm not sure, Mrs. Slatter.

She opened it where I had inserted a leaf to hold my place. Well, looks like you've just started.

She smiled and handed the book back to me and walked down the steps and over to Rosalind's tent, where she squatted down and pushed open the flap and said something I couldn't catch. There was a brief earnest conversation in low tones. Don't disappoint me, I heard her say as she stood up. She walked over to the larger tent and slipped inside. I had a good view of her calves throughout.

To my back came sounds of Mother banging around in the kitchen. With unusual suddenness black clouds rolled over the canyon from the east, though not so far as to block out the declining sun, about to slip behind the western ridge above the canyon. I wondered whether Mrs. Slatter, who was always so nice, carried around with her an invisible sack filled with private things like I knew Mother and Dad did, and Aunt Ruby, and probably even Walter, who was always anxious to please when he wasn't bored, or irritable about something, usually something Mickey had done. Mickey had that invisible sack, which contained his illegal firecrackers, a live .22 bullet, and until recently the little book of dirty pictures, and he walked around as if to show off that he had special things, as if he was becoming somebody, a person. And Rosalind's impenetrable screen of absentmindedness showed that she, too, had something no one else did, which she fed by the hour with all the books she went through; perhaps it was something you could get by reading. Yet how could I ask her? What were the words?

What I knew seemed paltry. I was too lethargic to enjoy the energetic hikes that other guests like the Slatters sometimes dragged me along on, hikes that always had to go to some destination, to the top of the canyon following an old Indian trail or the railroad tracks or down to the falls at the Sluice Box, whose thundering rapids into a long deep pool, turquoise blue where the water slowed, I found frightening. I much preferred a little path up behind the lodge that led through the boulders to a shelf where a trickle of water emerged from the ground to feed a miniature grassy meadow and little mounds of bright-green moss on rocks where the water disappeared back into the earth, and where on the way up I would follow the pale-green and orange and gray lichens that clung to the dark-brown boulders pocked with volcanic bubbles. Playmates I first led up there saw nothing—and would throw stones at the lizards or would want to scramble across the warm boulders to look at the larger spring, whose water flowed slowly into a cracked cement basin surrounded by a tangle of chicken wire to keep animals out; it supplied water to the lodge by way of a long rusty pipe. After a while the little meadow became a place I went to alone.

A peal of thunder rumbled over the canyon. Mrs. Slatter stepped out of her tent and zipped up the flap and went over and said something into Rosalind's. In a moment she, too, emerged, and the two of them fastened the snaps on the flap of the pup tent. Peter climbed out of the back of the Studebaker.

Did you roll the windows up?

No.

Well, go back and roll up the windows.

All of them?

One by one they tramped up the flagstone stairs and through the veranda.

Scotty's reading the book you read last year, said Mrs. Slatter as they walked past, but Rosalind paid no heed. I followed them into the dining room. Mother had set the place mats and silverware at one end of the long plank table.

What can I do to help? Mrs. Slatter called into the kitchen.

After a pause during which there was a small crash, Mother called back, Perhaps you could . . .

Mrs. Slatter carried plates in from the kitchen and told us where to sit, me next to Peter on one side, Rosalind opposite me and next to her mother on the other, Mother at the head of the table. When Mother brought in her own plate, we all sat down.

We ate in silence as the sky darkened and rumbled. Rosalind stared down at her plate as she picked up pieces of boiled potato with her fork, with thoughtful precision. Peter pushed his food around the plate, now and then placing the empty fork in his mouth and pretending to chew bites of meat.

After a while Mother muttered, The electricity will go out, of course.

Have you ever been up to the mine, Scotty? Mrs. Slatter asked me while discreetly wagging a finger at Peter. He forked a too-large piece of the roast into his mouth and began chewing laboriously.

Scotty Senior took him up once, Mother answered for me. He didn't like it.

I liked the train ride up to the 8,500-foot mine but when we got there the machinery was smoky and deafening and the men were dirty and gruff. Dad and I slept in a cold cabin on hard beds under blankets so crushingly heavy that I ached all over when I woke up. And my asthma came back.

Harold loves going up there.

The conversation died. Peter was making grotesque gestures with his jaw as he attempted to reduce the size of the lump of meat, face bright red. Then the lights went out, a few seconds before a deafening lightning strike somewhere nearby. The lodge got its electricity from the line that paralleled the railroad tracks but since we had no phone, sometimes days would go by before it went back on again. I would probably be sent up to the tracks tomorrow morning to hand a message up to Mr. Sanchez on the northbound train.

In the gloom Rosalind cast a panicked look in the direction of her mother. How am I going to read?

Scotty, could you do the lamps, please?

I got up and went over to the mantelpiece and struck a match and lifted one by one the glasses of the three kerosene lamps and lit them, letting them burn a minute before adjusting the wicks so they wouldn't smoke. I placed them evenly the length of the long table. Sensing I had an audience, I did this carefully without burning my fingers or getting kerosene on them or knocking over a lampshade. The sharp, sweetish odor of burning kerosene mingled with that of the more mellow pine smoke from the kitchen range. Outside a downpour began. The raindrops splashed white off the dark rocks. Puddles were already forming. There was still just enough light to see patches of the river through the trees, its surface pimpled with splashes and quickly merging concentric rings. A wave of cool damp air rolled in through the open doors and windows. The deep pounding of rain on the veranda roof suggested that this might be more than the usual downpour.

A real cloudburst, Mrs. Slatter observed. I hope the tents are all right.

Mother glanced up at the ceiling, as if to search out leaks, but the lodge had been re-roofed in red asphalt shingles two years before and, according to Dad, rendered tight for the first time since it was built in the late 1890s.

Mrs. Slatter got up from the table and went over to the veranda screen door and looked out. Oh dear, she said. The rest of us joined her. The large green tent where she and Mr. Slatter slept on cots seemed fine but the little brown pup tent had been set up within a barely perceptible depression. Muddy water appeared to be flowing inside, under a corner of the flap.

I suppose I had better go out. Do you have a raincoat, Irma?

Mother went to rummage around the closet under the staircase. The cottonwoods whipped by rain and wind were blanched by flashes of lightning, accompanied by staccato rolls of thunder and the occasional sharp crack as the lightning reached down into the canyon. The rain descended in erratic torrents. Mother came back with a poncho of heavy oiled canvas and a bright yellow rain hat, which Mrs. Slatter slipped on.

Do you think it's safe? Mother asked.

I just want to try to save their sleeping bags before they get soaked. She turned to Rosalind. Where's your book?

It was in her hand. She held it up. I knew she had kept it in her lap all through dinner. For the first time Rosalind seemed to be trying to take in what was going on around her and listening to what was said.

There will be a real good flood, I suggested with excessive enthusiasm. She stared at me, wide-eyed. Sometimes even the railroad tracks wash out.

What will happen to Daddy? Peter asked. He had been jumping up and down with excitement at the tumult outside but now stopped.

Mother looked at me and said, Scotty, for heaven's sake, don't even think of that.

It's true. It did last year, I insisted. And sometimes huge boulders come crashing down.

Scotty, please.

Rosalind stared at me as if examining my features and expressions for the first time. I hoped it would rain and rain and the river flood so high it would almost reach the house and that boulders would crash down into the water and that trees would be struck by lightning. After it was all over I would walk her through the muddy aftermath and show her the dead fish along the bank, the uprooted trees, how the boulders had been thrown around.

Did the train crash? Peter wanted to know.

Mrs. Slatter was out the door and running hunched over down the steps. She fumbled with the tent flap and pushed it aside and leaned inside and grabbed up the sleeping bags and balled them up with such violence I thought she was going to rip out the stakes and bring the tent down. She stuffed them under the poncho as best she could and ran back up the steps and stopped just under the porch. Mother opened the screen door and took the sleeping bags while Mrs. Slatter shed the dripping poncho and hat, spreading them out on the swing-sofa to dry, and pulled off her sopping canvas shoes. Her rain-splashed honey-colored calves glistened in the gloom. In the living room Mother spread the sleeping bags out over the furniture. They smelled of the tent canvas. Soon the two women were going over the dark-green flannel to see if there were any wet patches. Other than being damp in places from the dash through the rain, they were dry.

We finished dinner as the rain continued to beat down. It stopped as abruptly as it started. Lightning flashes grew fainter in the far distance to the west. Through the sound of water dripping from the eaves and the cottonwoods came the low rumble of the river rising, and soon the muffled banging of boulders being loosened and rolled in the swollen current. In a moment the peculiar smell of flooding, a sharp musty mixture of dry pine needles and clay, drifted into the lodge.

Would you and Rosalind please do the dishes? Mother asked,

stacking dessert plates and gathering up silverware. I moved two of the kerosene lamps into the kitchen and placed them on the windowsill above the sink. Mother and Mrs. Slatter carried in the dishes and straightened up the counter and stove in the semi-darkness. Mother slid a log into the firebox and opened the air control.

A glass of sherry, Louise? Mother asked with the first smile of the evening, but with a pursing of the lips that indicated she was trying to be polite. I'm going to have one. Would you care to join me?

Wash or dry? I asked Rosalind, who was contemplating with a nervous twitch of her eyes the simple wooden sink counter stained black around the edges of the white enamel basin and the single tap made out of an outdoor faucet with a brass handle to which a few chips of red paint still adhered. Mother poured a teakettle of hot water into the basin, turned on the tap, and rubbed a large bar of Ivory into some suds.

Dry, I guess, she replied. Mother handed her a dish towel. I was in a state of rapture. This was the first question of mine that Rosalind had ever answered. I stopped myself from repeating it.

Just a taste, said Mrs. Slatter.

Through the kitchen window over the sink there was normally visible a sliver of the river as it washed around a huge slide of dark boulders. Through the reflection of the lamps, now all I could see was that the water level was higher, with edges of the water made lighter by mud and clay marked by a white line of foam along the rocks. Now and then a dark shape floated past. See, logs, huge logs, I said. I pulled the window open. The kitchen was hot and steamy. Cool fragrant air flowed in. Rosalind strained to see.

Where?

Wait. There. See that one?

Oh.

I want to see, Peter said, tugging at my sleeve.

Mrs. Slatter moved a kitchen chair over and he climbed up on it, towering over us. I began washing silverware according to Aunt Ruby's ironclad formula of silverware first, glasses second, plates and bowls third, most cookware fourth, and frying pans the very last of all. If you can't remember which comes first, young man—the *young man* was interchangeably Mickey or me—then just think of which items touch your mouth and which don't. You start with what touches your mouth. You finish with what touches the stove. Very, very last, what touches the floor, if anything happens to.

Whenever Peter spotted a log or a tree, or more often than not when he thought he did, he alerted us.

I washed away happily, chest bursting at having my first real conversation with Rosalind, no matter that on her side it consisted of a few monosyllables. Mother had pulled open the silverware drawer and the cupboard door above it, so Rosalind would know where things went once I had washed and rinsed them under the cold tap and set them down on a dish towel spread out on the wooden counter. I washed with the dainty precision of what I imagined to be expert gestures, letting my long bony hands linger over the rinsed utensils and dishes as I laid them down on the towel, so that she might admire them—as Aunt Ruby had once done, picking them up one by one and spreading my fingers out on her palm and looking down at them critically before making her pronouncement, Good hands, you'll have good hands. Mickey will, too, not that it will help, she said, as if imagining all the trouble his hands would get him into.

Mother and Mrs. Slatter had moved back to the living room. I was conscious of the burning presence in the dim orange light to my left, a blur out of the corner of my eye, which I knew stood for a white blouse with an embroidered seam, mysteriously puffed out in front without, I sensed, much solid behind it, and a tiny gold locket on a gold chain around her neck, and glasses with heavy black rims pointed upward where the earpieces attached, her downcast dark eyes concentrating on the silverware and glasses, the flicks of the ragged gray dish towel.

Peter got tired of standing on the chair and peering into the darkness outside. In the course of climbing down he pulled me toward Rosalind and caused our bare elbows to touch exactly where my scar was. She recoiled. I looked down. Holding my elbow up and with a wet finger I pointed to the dime-sized disk, darker and shinier than the surrounding skin.

I got that when I broke my arm in third grade.

She glanced down at it for the briefest of moments, then went back to drying silverware.

How?

A friend pushed me. Well, he pushed me and I fell over backward and broke my arm. That's from the cast. He had a glass eye.

I was unable to follow this revelation with more daring details, such as how Paul used to pop out the blue eye and slip it into his mouth and roll it around and then open his lips. I was out of breath from what I had already confessed.

Peter had wandered back to the living room. I could hear

Mother explaining something to Mrs. Slatter. From her tone of voice I guessed it was about how she consented to spend summers at the lodge only to keep Dad happy and how exasperated she was at the electricity failures and the lack of fresh fruit and vegetables most of the time and no telephone and how she counted the days before they would get in the car and head back down to Denver. I had overheard countless times these details confided to wives of family friends after dinner over port or sherry or brandy or in the afternoon over tea or coffee whenever the men were out, either up at the mine or fishing down below the Sluice Box. It was almost as if she would go into a trance and it would all pour out, except in the presence of Aunt Ruby. Then Mother would become quiet and complain about her health. By her own account Aunt Ruby had silenced Mother not long after she and Dad were married, when Mother had tried to complain to her about the long summers in the canyon. You should have known, Irma, that when you married Scotty you were also marrying the lodge. The phrase stuck in my memory because I had no idea for a long time what *marrying the lodge* could possibly mean. There were variations throughout the years, the most common replacing *the lodge* with *the mine*, both of which were subcategories of her more general dictum, When you marry the man you should be clear about what else you are marrying.

The river was loud now and the rich odor of flotsam suggested that it was becoming an excellent flood, of a strength that would completely rearrange the landscape at the beach.

I sprained my ankle once, Rosalind confided to the open window.

How?

Falling off my mother's bike.

What kind of bike was it? I blurted out, betraying my priorities.

A grown-up's bike, she said.

I had finished the plates. I looked at the pots, one of them sticky with mashed potatoes. I wondered whether I could get away with soaking it. I was in a state of overexcitement and exhaustion at what was now feeling like a conversation of interminable length, with far too many questions branching off into so many shadowy paths, none of which would stay fixed long enough for me to voice. Bike? Fall? Mother? I imagined the scene: the girl sprawled on the dirt, tangled up in the tall bicycle, a dog with a long drooling tongue standing and staring off to one side, a car stopping and a man and a woman dashing across the street, in a town I had never been to: Pomona, California. I pulled out the drain plug, then immediately regretted it, wondering if I could find more dishes to wash. To our backs came the slamming sound of the veranda screen door.

Down at the tents Mrs. Slatter was playing a flashlight beam over the scene. After a moment she dragged the air mattresses out of the pup tent and up into the veranda to dry. The big tent, she told us when she came back inside with bare feet, was still dry and she would be able to sleep there tonight, but the pup tent was a sopping mess.

Rosalind and Peter can sleep in Scotty's room, Mother announced. I'll put Scotty in one of the empty rooms across the hall.

I was relieved. I was getting nervous at the thought of all three of us sleeping in the same room. I went back to the kitchen and carried out the other two kerosene lamps and set them on the dining table with the other one. Their absence would usefully obscure the fact I hadn't washed the pots.

Oh good, Mrs. Slatter said, there's enough light for the two of you to read.

Rosalind was already at the table with her book spread open. I went and got mine from the veranda and sat down opposite her. She was reading quickly and smoothly, her eyes gliding down the page, up to the top of the next, even though the print was very small. What's the book? I asked.

She looked up at me coldly. *War and Peace.*

I am so impressed, I heard Mother say from her armchair in the living room, where she had lit a fire. I'm so impressed at Rosalind's reading. I do worry about Scotty Junior spending summers here without all the exciting things you can do in Chicago or even Denver for that matter. She was starting up again, I suspected.

I knew nothing yet of Tolstoy but was fascinated at how Rosalind could so completely block out her surroundings by reading—even though I was about to do exactly the same. But as I read and became lost in the words and images and conversations on the page I still glanced up every now and then to make certain she was still there across the faint hissing of the flames, within the halo of odiferous light from the lamps that enclosed us. Later into the evening it came to feel as if we were in a kind of race, not to see who could finish their book first, since both volumes seemed too dense and fat to ever quite finish, but to see which of us could hold out the longest, read the farthest, sail the most distantly off into some other world, remote and inaccessible to others. In the darkness outside the river roared unabated. Now and then a cool breeze would carry its earthy odor into the room, mingle with the scent of burning pine. The women chatted with growing lethargy. Peter squirmed on the couch next to his mother. I'm bored, he whined. As I read I half-consciously wove all these strands—the smelly kerosene lamps, the big old house, Rosalind reading across the table, the river—into the story of Jude, my surroundings becoming features of that imagined scene, its encounters, conversations, the English countryside, inappropriate angles softened and blurred, pushed off into corners, yet still there, on the edges, in the shadows, as if in entering into these exotic landscapes through the act of reading I could not help but drag my present life along, behind the thin beam of consciousness that illuminated and unlocked word and sentence and paragraph and page. As I turned the pages one at a time I became transfixed by how they emerged out of the darkness from the right to glow in the light of the lamps, even radiating a faint heat up into my downturned face, and then after an interval of reading how I would consign them back into darkness to the left, where they would remain sealed up until the next reader pulled the volume from the shelf, reopened it, and began to read.

Time passed, perhaps an hour, perhaps more. I was aware of Mother getting up and taking one of the lamps into the kitchen and pouring herself some more sherry and replacing the lamp on the table and returning to the armchair beside the fireplace. In response to Mrs. Slatter's questions, the conversation had turned to the absent husbands and then the mine and its long and convoluted history, most of whose twists and turns I had overheard so many times in these after-dinner conversations (though I was some years away from beginning to understand the intricacies of the situation) that I considered them ordinary and of little interest: how Dad's grandfather had gained a controlling interest in the mine but then had almost lost it during a market crash, after which things had always been up and down. I had no idea what a market crash was, nor did I understand how the war had kept the mine alive another five years through the extraction of a mineral or rare earth—beryllium?—that had been of little value but suddenly proved to be of use in the manufacture of radio vacuum tubes during the war. But it was clear to me in these conversations, particularly when Mother unburdened herself to another woman while Dad was away, that nothing good was ever going to come of the mine operation, which my painful visit at age six seemed to confirm. More than once, Mother confided, Scotty's sister Ruby has had to help us out. This, too, I knew (though not yet the extent), having once overheard a conversation around the family dining table in Denver, during which Aunt Ruby had said, As you know perfectly well, money always goes to the women because we don't have the means to earn it. That's why, Scotty dear, you have ended up with the wretched mine. But I'll help you when I can.

What was new in this evening's exchange was that in between Mother's laments about how much Dad worried about the business and how bad it was for her health to spend summers at the lodge, Mrs. Slatter interjected comments that seemed to be saying that Harold, her husband, was himself much less sanguine about the prospects of the operation than he used to be. He and Dad and Mrs. Slatter had gone to college together. According to Aunt Ruby, Dad had even briefly dated Mrs. Slatter despite the fact that he was a head shorter. She was smart, that one, Aunt Ruby once said to me, to marry the geologist, not the owner of the mine. Mines come and go but geology is forever. This, like many of Aunt Ruby's pronounce-ments, took me several years to puzzle out.

Rosalind kept on reading with quick and decisive flips of the page. My state of excitement at so much concentration divided between the words on the page and Rosalind reading right across the table was winding up to the snapping point. Occasional yawns were coming from the women. The ormolu clock on the mantelpiece was working tonight: it read half past nine. Mrs. Slatter kept twisting her head around to look at Rosalind, perhaps to see whether she dared interrupt her read-ing. Finally she did.

Another fifteen minutes, Rosalind protested without look-ing up.

No, we're all tired. And there will be no reading by flash-light in your room, either. We need to save the batteries.

What about the lamps?

No, you cannot take kerosene lamps to bed, young lady.

Lamps and sleeping bags in hand, redolent of tent canvas and kerosene smoke, we all tramped upstairs to my room, where Mother pulled off my sleeping bag and carried it across the hall to one of the three unused rooms that was kept more or less clean for such emergencies and dumped it on a mattress on the floor. Back in my room Rosalind and Peter were squab-bling over who was going to get the top bunk. Rosalind won. Besides, he's just a baby, she said, he'll fall out of bed. Before going back downstairs the women left one of the lamps on the hallway floor for us to see by through our half-open doors and asked me to put out the light before I went to bed. I changed into my pajamas in the empty half-dark room.

Stop looking, Peter.

I can't see anything.

I heard the bed creak as Rosalind climbed into the top bunk.

Stop bouncing up and down. You'll make it fall over.

After a few other altercations the room fell silent and I stepped out the door and turned down the wick. The flame shrank down to a blue strip and I blew it out. I felt my way back into the room and slipped into my sleeping bag. I imagined Rosalind lying awake up in my bunk, her body slipping into the depression I had worn into the lumpy kapok mattress. She would be wiggling around to make herself comfortable, tossing this way and then that and trying to make out forms in the strange room. I knew the space intimately: the little wooden rails, stained dark red, that were supposed to keep you from falling out of bed but pressed too close in the narrow bunk; the low plank ceiling, whose fur-like roughness you could reach up to, propped up on an elbow, and touch; the smoother tongue-and-groove wall, to which was attached a small shelf where I kept the comic books I no longer bothered to look through. My face flushed as I realized that in the morning light Rosalind would undoubtedly reach up there to see what they were, pick one up, disdainfully put it back. Or perhaps not. Perhaps she wouldn't even notice them. I went back to imagining her shifting around in my bed, warming its space, staring out the open window facing the cottonwoods and still-throaty river, at the tattered Mexican rug on the floor with its zigzag weave, at the gray porcelain light fixture and bare bulb in the center of the ceiling, all of it dimly illuminated by the blue-gray light of a starry sky. I wondered whether she would be lying there, as I so often did, trying to make sense of distant snatches of conversation and laughter of the adults, though tonight the women downstairs were either quiet or inaudible; or perhaps she was listening to the noises of the old house, the creakings and crackings, the tickings and scrapings from above, probably from the feral cat prowling around the attic, the rustlings and scratchings that came through the window, the always-mysterious *bang* from up on the rail line late at night. Or would she be running over the lines and pages of what she had read during the day, heedless of her surroundings, not caring or even aware that she was sleeping tonight in my room, in my bed? Did she sleep with her glasses on? The image of her lying there for perhaps only this one night thrilled me and helped me adapt to my own new and disorienting surroundings, which I hardly noticed as I lay there for what seemed like hours, eyes half-open, ears straining to pick up the slightest sound from across the hall. I remembered the spell was broken only for an instant when Mother tiptoed up the stairs and down the hall and closed her noisy bedroom door. A minute later I heard the screen door downstairs open and close, footsteps down the flagstone steps, the long zipping sound of Mrs. Slatter opening her tent flap. Rosalind, I was certain, cradled by my dreaming concentration from across the hall, slept through it all.

It was broad daylight when I awoke. The sun had crested the ridge and was glaring into the room. Mother was calling up the stairs. Scotty, remember you have to take a note up to the train. I scrambled to my feet and pulled on my clothes. I thought I would be the last one up but it appeared that Rosalind and Peter were still asleep in my room, or so I thought. The women were downstairs sitting at the dining room table and sipping coffee. I stepped out onto the veranda. Through the cottonwoods it appeared that the sand of the beach had been covered with a layer of reddish clay. A tower of driftwood had jammed up against the boulders I often sat on. The water flowed milky reddish brown. If the sky didn't cloud up again the water would be unusually warm by early afternoon. I loved paddling around in the silky water despite the adults' expressions of distaste. It was all right as long as I rinsed myself off afterward with the ice-cold spring water from the pipe behind the house. Usually I cheated, just giving my face a quick smear.

I wanted to show the scene off to Rosalind. While waiting for her to come down, I sat down at the table, and Mother served me a breakfast of cornflakes, which we were running out of, and toast. Rosalind's book was gone from the far end of the long table, where I had last seen it before going to bed. Mother was telling Mrs. Slatter how she particularly disliked this part of the summer when the rains came and the road sometimes became impassable and invariably the electricity went off, sometimes for a week at a time. If it didn't come back on today, we'd have to move all of the food out of the refrigerator into a cave dug out behind the shed that used to serve as an icehouse, guarded by a screened-off cage that kept the mice out. I interrupted to ask were Rosalind was.

She got up early, Mrs. Slatter said, and went back up to your room to read after she had breakfast. I hope that's all right.

At that moment Peter jumped down from the third step with a crash. She won't ever let me into the top bunk, he pouted.

This presented a new and unexpected problem. I had dreamed the night away imagining her sleeping in the top bunk, and now I wondered how to dislodge her and get her outside away from her book so I could show off the wonders of the flood's aftermath. If I went up and just asked her, she would say no. I gulped down my breakfast and stood up and took my plate and bowl and silverware into the kitchen and set them down on the counter without making a sound, then came around the other way into the dining room and picked up my book without the women paying attention—Mrs. Slatter was trying to talk Peter into eating something—and climbed up the stairs. The hallway smelled of pine, suggesting it might be a hot day. Wordlessly I slipped into my room and pushed Peter's sleeping bag aside and lay down and opened my book. It was almost too dark to read in the lower bunk. Rosalind must have noticed my arrival and mysterious behavior because she shifted back and forth above me. The striped mattress, held in place by thin metal straps, sagged in the middle under her weight. I began reading. I heard a page turn above me. For perhaps fifteen minutes the only sounds in the room were her turning a page, then me, then her again. The wood ceiling creaked as it warmed. Finally I blurted out the burning question: Do you want to go down to the river and look at the flood?

But hot on my words, Mother called up the stairs. Scotty, where are you? The train's due in twenty minutes.

I had forgotten. I climbed out of bed and ran down the stairs. Mother handed me the envelope. Be careful, she said.

Can I come? Peter asked with a whine.

You haven't eaten your breakfast, Peter.

I ran out the back door and up the path to the spring. The clay was still slippery from the rain and I had to jump from rock to rock and step only on the gravelly patches.

51

From way down in the canyon came the sound of the whistle. Normally I would have enjoyed the errand, which made me feel important, but this time I was worried that Rosalind would go down to the river herself or with Peter and cast a quick eye over the scene and turn away from it without seeing the fascinating details I would be sure to point out. Or Peter would start throwing mud at her. The path to the tracks switchbacked 150 feet or so up through the boulders, with two narrow patches just wide enough to squeeze through, and along a ledge of rock I was afraid to look down from, before giving way to a short sandy track, not steep, that led up to the railroad cut in the side of the steep slope of the canyon wall. A few rocks had been washed down into the path and lay on ribbons of freshly washed sand. I got up to the tracks just as a motorized handcar manned by two men in overalls chugged past up the hill. They waved, called out something I couldn't understand. Dad said that sometimes the railroad sent a handcar ahead of the train to check that the tracks were okay.

I stood and waited. Below, the river waters had receded to just above normal, the muddy flow lazy and peaceful before it funneled into the churning dirty brown rapids that stepped down toward the Sluice Box. From above, the massive lodge looked small, its pitched roof of dark-red asphalt shingles resembling a giant patch of lichen or some other growth among the charcoal-brown boulders, a strand of gray smoke wafting from the smaller of its stone chimneys. Peter and Mrs. Slatter were out front, looking down at the partially collapsed pup tent. The chrome of the two-tone gray Studebaker gleamed in the sun. The contours of the canyon walls now and then directed random sounds of the slowly ascending but still-distant train in my direction, in brief pulses, over the murmurs of the river below: the clanking of the drive-wheel rods, the hiss of escaping steam, chains and hitches banging and rattling, almost-musical sounds breaking through the explosive clamor of the locomotive laboring up the steep grade. I was worried as usual about being spotted with soot. From its position high up on the side of the canyon I estimated that the train was still fifteen to twenty minutes away. I sat down on a rock, irked that Mother had sent me up early. Why hadn't she waited for the sound of the whistle?

Down below, Mrs. Slatter had gone back inside the lodge. A minute later she emerged with Rosalind and gestured to her and Peter to help her with the pup tent. The three of them dragged it up the stone steps, perhaps to drain out the water. Various articles of clothing had already been spread out on the rocks to dry. Once they got the tent positioned on one side of the steps, Mrs. Slatter propped it open with the tentpoles. Rosalind tried to go back into the house; but, arms waving, Mrs. Slatter directed her to carry the wet clothing around to the back and hang it on the line, then sent Peter after her with the rest. Or so I guessed. From where I was sitting, the clothesline was hidden beneath the brow of the slope. Sooner or later Mother would probably rush outside and tell them to bring the bedding inside until after the locomotive passed.

Time dragged. There were so many more exciting things to do than wait for the train. I hadn't even gone down to the river yet. Dramatic snags of driftwood jammed against boulders littered the stretch I could see and there were even clumps of twigs high up into the branches of willows in protected little bays. I stood up and walked up and down the tracks in search of interesting pieces of metal that now and then fell off passing trains.

The rains had washed away bits of toilet paper and newspaper and mysterious white lumps of cloth that sometimes littered the tracks from the toilet at the end of the passenger car. Until I was five or six I hadn't made the obvious connection between the moment I flushed the toilet on a moving train, opening a fascinating hole beneath which the wooden ties whizzed by, and the receiving ground, as if the very motion of the train somehow made everything go away, which in a relative sense it did; the connection finally came when I was playing on the tracks one afternoon while waiting for the train and Dad called out, Hey, son, watch out for the turds. One of the first phrases I learned to read was *Do Not Flush Toilet While Train Is Standing in Station*, with its many mysterious meanings, none of which the adults were willing to explicate. Despite my somewhat more advanced knowledge now, I was still fascinated with it all, with the steel rails themselves and their somehow emblematic cross section of a flat foot, a long thin column holding up the wafer-shaped top of the rail, its upper surface polished where the wheels rumbled along it, flaked and scored along the edges on curves, and the dirty steel plates and spikes that held them down to the splintering crossties black with creosote, and the rigid yet fluid geometry of a rail line as it cut through and around features of landscapes that would have seemed random and chaotic without it. A touch of that old excitement came back to me while I sauntered up and down the tracks, whose rails gleamed in the morning sun through smears of rust brought on by last night's rain. I picked up a rusty spike and slipped it into my back pocket.

At last the steam-snorting silver snout of the engine waddled around the bend. I raised my hand and waved the envelope. The engineer gave a quick toot of the whistle. After a moment, Mr. Sanchez leaned out of the baggage car door, went back inside, reappeared on the front platform, stepped down to the lowermost step.

There's no electricity, I called up to Mr. Sanchez as he leaned over to take the letter.

No surprise given that storm, he called back. We'll get it on again.

That afternoon Mother sent me back up the tracks to wait for the southbound train. The lights had still not come on. Ask Mr. Sanchez, Mother said, if they have any idea when. The morning and half the afternoon had passed without Rosalind wanting to tear herself away from her book except to go to the bathroom and eat half a sandwich for lunch. At one point, in desperation I ran down to the beach and had a quick look at the changes the flood had wrought, on my way back to the house thinking up ways to exaggerate the effects of the flood enough to compel Rosalind to drop her reading. But by then the sound of the whistle at the top of the canyon told me it was about time to go back up to the tracks.

Usually the train descended at seven or eight miles an hour, by Dad's estimate, but this time it seemed to be moving more slowly. The brakes squealed. To my surprise the train came to a shuddering halt just before the last car reached me. Dad and Mr. Slatter, suitcases in hand, swung down from the rear passenger car. I ran up to greet them.

There's no electricity, I said to Dad.

I know. Sanchez told me.

The line's down in about four places, Mr. Sanchez said. Maybe in a day or two.

With a lurch the train resumed rolling.

I followed the two men as they slipped and jumped down the slope. Up at the mine the storm had been even worse. They had been up all night trying to deal with some flooding. They were surprised that no landslides had closed the rail line. I told them about the pup tent. Dad looked ashen, seemed tired. At one point on the way down the steep slope, just before the lodge, they stopped. Mr. Slatter was first. He turned around and looked up and said with his usual cheerful tone, Look, Scotty, not even the best of us can tell you what's down there. Sure, the south tunnel's probably gone for good but there could be something on either side.

Dad shook his head but said nothing. One by one we felt our way along the short ledge and then bounded down the steep path to the next clump of boulders and finally down the gentler slope to the back of the lodge, where we tramped in the back door to the kitchen. The women set down dishes and napkins they were about to put away.

Mrs. Slatter embraced her husband. I thought you were going to stay two nights, she said.

No point really, Dad muttered. One was enough.

Is everything all right? Mother asked. Whenever they parted or reunited after an absence, Mother would hesitantly touch Dad's forearm, nothing more, at least in my presence. Even Aunt Ruby, verbally demonstrative, only issued quick pecks on the cheek, often followed by a dry, Well, we got that over with, didn't we? The Slatters' embraces seemed like something out of the movies.

We'll talk about it later, Dad said. This was a signal that the adults wanted to talk over something alone, out of earshot of children, usually to do with real estate or investments, which were still mysterious concepts to me. In a new suburb not far from our Denver house there was a tiny house, a shack really, which sat kitty-corner at an intersection. A sign above the porch read *Reed Realty*. This puzzled me for the longest time. Adults never used the term *realty*. Eventually I learned that a Mr. Reed somehow owned Reed Realty. But what could be meant by *Reed Realty*? I knew that people owned things, including houses and land. Very occasionally cars were bought and sold but not houses, at least not in my then-young experience. For a long time the little shack that housed Reed Realty stood for all I didn't understand about the adult world. Once I even leaned my bike against the railing and walked up the steps to the porch and peered in the open door. Mr. Reed was smoking and talking on the phone at a small desk. He had a big jaw and a very lined red face. A tall dark-green war-surplus filing cabinet stood at the other end of the small room. Hanging from the wall was a calendar illustrated with a painting of an English racing horse, or so I later worked out, in front of a white wooden fence. That was all.

Rosalind was back in my bunk reading. I sat down on the lower bunk. My return from my second trip up the hill elicited no notice. I suppressed an urge to lie back on the lower bed and raise my legs and give the bulge above a good kick—as I had done at least three times a day when Mickey was up there.

Let's go down to the river and look at the flood, I called up with a firm and slightly cross voice. It's getting late. There could be another storm.

I have to finish this chapter first, she called back mechanically.

Why?

Because I have to, that's all. He's about to propose.

Who?

I can't pronounce their names.

I threw myself down on the bed. The bulge above shifted. Then it appeared to stretch in some strange way, the gray mattress ticking slipping from side to side, the little tie strings jiggling. Then it bounced once. I stared up at the gray bulge and waited for it to reveal its next transformation. We were close, within touching distance at least, which was something. Would I have to lie here on my back all day? I had heard the argument before, I have to finish this chapter first, whenever Mrs. Slatter asked her to do something. Unless her mother nagged her several times the "chapter" would stretch out to an hour or more. I opened my book but it was dark in the lower bunk and I didn't really feel like reading anyway, so I slammed the book closed. The bulge did not move. I realized I hadn't yet seen close up what the flood had done and immediately became agitated. What should I do?

I stood up and threw my book on the bed. You'd better come and see the flood before it's too late, I said. Rosalind was rolled over on her side with her back toward me.

Will you just let me finish this chapter?

I walked out of the room and down the stairs. This was hurting. With my friends who were boys, the problem was finding time away from them. They were all restless, wanting to do things all the time, and since the lodge and the canyon were in varying degrees new for them, I had to be the guide. After a day with Cousin Mickey or any of the others my face was hot and flushed and I often wanted to go hide—and occasionally did, up near the spring or down behind the boulders at the lower end of the beach. They would ask, Where did you go? Nowhere. With Rosalind I was doing something wrong.

Downstairs the women were carrying food from the dripping refrigerator out the back door and through the shed to the ice-house cave in the side of hill. The men were sitting and smoking on the veranda with Mr. Slatter's geological sketches spread out over the wicker table but were staring outside at nothing in particular. I went outside. Peter emerged from somewhere.

He called after me, Where are you going?

Nowhere.

Can I come along?

I ignored him but he tagged along anyway, down through the cottonwoods to the beach, where a thick new layer of small rocks and fine sand had been deposited. At the water's edge there was a wide band of reddish mud and black pine needles and small piñon cones and short branches and roots worn smooth by their travels through the rocky gorge. The water still flowed creamy brown but was almost down to its normal level. Small rocks and driftwood littered my favorite boulders, and a tent-like structure of logs and roots had been pushed up against them at the end of the beach. Look, I would have said to Rosalind, look at those logs and what the flood has done to them, you could hardly lift them they're so heavy. And see that rock there, I would have pointed to the center of the flow, the flood must have moved it twenty feet downstream. Though in fact I wondered whether it had moved at all. For Rosalind I would exaggerate. I felt proprietary toward this short section of the river and knew its details by heart. Peter was squishing his bare feet around in the soft mud. I wanted to tell him to stop. Later when the mud would dry out and curl up into potato chip–like forms, I liked to gather them up and toss them into the almost-clear water and watch the plumes of muddiness trail them as they tumbled and dissolved deep in the flow. I was about to say something when there was a shout to my back.

Daddy says we have to leave.

Rosalind was standing at the edge of the sand. I have to pack my things, she said. Peter, get out of the mud and rinse off your filthy feet. She was squinting through her glasses, her nose slightly upturned as if sniffing the rich new smell of the drying mud and pine needles. It seemed pointless to show off the flood to her now. I wasn't surprised the Slatters were leaving so soon: there was always talk of their staying for a week or more but they never did. A new round of thunderheads was building up over the east side of the canyon. This early meant more rain. I had plans to show Rosalind my secret little meadow and take her into the water near the boulder just above where the low rapids began, even up to the tracks to wait for the train, though I still had no idea how to lure her away from her reading and focus her eyes on things more than a few inches from her face.

Peter rinsed off his feet and dragged them through the wet sand and followed her back through the cottonwoods, mud still crusted to his ankles. She had been sent down to get him, not to find me. I scrambled across the rocks to one of my favorite basalt boulders and pushed aside the debris of sticks and pebbles and sat down. Up in front of the lodge the Studebaker doors were open and Mr. Slatter was piling stuff into the trailer. The green tent began to collapse. Mrs. Slatter stepped outside and patted it down into a flat shape. I was already beginning to miss Rosalind and feel lonely. I imagined her riding back to Pomona in the backseat of the two-tone Studebaker, reading away, squabbling with Peter. I would write her secret letters, which she would secretly read. She loved to read, she couldn't help but read, she might not listen to me but she would certainly read my letters. Somehow I would have to find her address in Mother's desk back in Denver, steal some postage stamps. I would tell her to make up a return address like *The Argus Stamp Collecting Company* because the only mail I got, other than birthday cards from Aunt Ruby, who always enclosed a brand-new dollar bill, was from stamp-collecting companies wanting me to send for their latest "approval" packages of stamps. But the problem with that subterfuge was that I had stopped buying stamps by mail because the company had taken to sending me packages of stamps worth ten and twenty dollars, values that frightened me. Mother had twice intervened, asking the stamp companies to stop sending stamps on approval to her son. Seeing such a letter, she'd ask, Are those companies still pestering you? But there must be a way. People were always writing secretly to each other in movies, getting messages across enemy lines.

Up at the lodge the bell clanged. Mother was shouting something down in my direction. I got up and ran across the beach and up through the cottonwoods. The Slatter car and trailer appeared to be mostly packed. I called for you to say good-bye, Mother said when I approached. Mr. Slatter was cinching down the canvas over the trailer, on top of which the pup tent had been spread out to dry between the ropes and the canvas cover. Mrs. Slatter was peering into the trunk, which, unlike my family, they called the *turtleback*. The kids were sitting in the backseat. Rosalind was reading. It was, I remembered, our book. She would have to mail it back. It would have been so easy to slip a letter into the pages. Why hadn't I thought of this before? I could have scribbled something and placed the sheet between pages 299 and 300 for her to find on her way home. Now and then she had left the book lying on the table. But now it was too late. I stood back, staring into the glamorous car, its interior soft with striped velour.

I paid little attention to the adults' farewells. Dad huddled briefly with Mr. Slatter. I overheard him say that normally it took two days to get a telegram up here unless we happened to be at the station in Basalt Junction when it came in.

Mother gave Mrs. Slatter a quick little handshake. Rosalind, prompted by her mother, shouted, Bye!, without looking up from her book. Peter leaned out the window and smiled and waved as if to a friendly crowd.

They pulled away from the lodge just as the first black clouds blotted out the late-afternoon sun. I hoped that it would rain and rain, generating an even bigger flood that would transform the river, even uproot a few cottonwood trees. *Dear Rosalind*, I would write, *You should have seen the next flood. It was*—I tried to think of a word that would describe the imagined cataclysm ahead.

Mother and Dad went back inside. I stood listening to the

sound of the Studebaker engine roaring up the steep part of the dirt drive, the clack of gravel hitting fenders and bumpers, the bang of the trailer hitch, the slap of its swinging safety chain. When the car had attained the flatter section of the road up at the tracks and Mr. Slatter had shifted into second gear, the engine quieted.

The sound grew faint and blended into the hiss of the river.

Three

THE WEEK PASSED slowly after the Slatters left. The electricity came back on the next day. There were no more floods. In between bouts of reading I pined for Rosalind as I lay on the sand on the beach and perched on various boulders in the water and sat on the edge of my private little meadow up on the hillside behind the lodge, and lounged on the top bunk bed, on the veranda swing. Within a few days her features blurred and faded and then coalesced into the sagging bulge of gray mattress I had contemplated from the lower bunk during our moments of greatest intimacy. I went to sleep, awoke, daydreamed with the bulge hanging over me, a distended fruit clad in striped gray mattress ticking, white threads almost imperceptibly jiggling: my Rosalind.

Dad went back up to the mine for most of the week. Mother wrote letters, took naps that lasted all afternoon, stayed up late knitting, got up later and later in the morning. Her attitude toward me was both absent and fretful as she made halfhearted attempts to anticipate my needs. Aren't you cold? Where's your jacket? I was used to making my own breakfast but a sandwich could appear anytime in the afternoon, and dinner got later and later. I hoped Dad would get back soon. He had arranged for Mr. Smedley to send groceries up on the train so Mother wouldn't have to drive the LaSalle down to Basalt Junction, but the cardboard box Mr. Sanchez stepped off the train with was so big that I had to divide the contents in two and make another trip up and down the side of the hill. I finished reading the Hardy, an accomplishment that surprised me, and moved on to Samuel Butler's *The Way of All Flesh*, which I was making much less sense of, starting with the title, whose meaning registered only several years later. For the time being, *flesh* tentatively stood for the gray bulge, close but unattainable.

The Nesbitts should arrive in a day or two, Mother said to me late the night before Dad was supposed to return. Her tone was of faint exasperation. So you'll have someone to play with.

Dad and Mother had known the Nesbitts a long time but only recently had they moved into our Denver neighborhood. Their son Frank was proving to be a bully at school though he had not yet turned his attentions to me. I had so far avoided him on the way to school by leaving the house early and riding my bike the long way, avoiding his street. After school, I spent time with friends living closer to school before riding home. I had seen what Frank could do to kids smaller and weaker than he was. He probably exempted me because our dads did business with each other.

Mr. and Mrs. Nesbitt were short and plump and boastful. Mr. Nesbitt owned a big company that distributed fuel oil and coal and wholesaled construction materials. Its oil tanks and piles of coal and gravel and steel beams down along the railroad tracks were objects of fascination whenever we drove past them on our way in or out of town. Dad had already done business with Mr. Nesbitt for several years when they moved into the largest house in the neighborhood, one of the first to be built after the war.

Why do we have to have these people up here? Mother wearily asked Dad the night he returned home, sliding the note from Mrs. Nesbitt across the table when they were sipping their after-dinner coffee.

Dad glanced at it, folded it up, slipped it back into the envelope. Horace kept insisting, he said. He gives me a break on steel and cement. During the war he was the only one I could get anything at all from.

I don't mind him so much, she said, not completing the thought when she realized I was still in the living room, slouched down on the couch and pretending to read. Had Aunt Ruby been there she would have halted the conversation by pronouncing loudly, Little pitchers have big ears. Until I was a certain age I took this personally. I had no idea what the saying meant but I knew I had big ears and therefore thought it must apply to me and me alone. My ears stuck out and turned bright red at the slightest provocation, adding to my agony. But I had reached an age where adults no longer made such remarks, they just abruptly fell silent.

But Mother couldn't help herself. It's Roberta I can't stand, she said. Please spend as little time as you can with him up at the mine.

He's been talking of investing in it.

Mother remained silent for a moment. Surely there must be others.

We may have no choice, Irma. But we'll talk about it later.

Later meant out of my hearing. And much later I learned that Mrs. Nesbitt reminded Mother of her older sister, too bossy, too old country, whom I finally met toward the end of her life, the family having dispersed following the death of their mother at a young age. I was well out of college before I finally became aware of the existence of Mother's side of the family, about whom she never spoke.

The Nesbitts' big dark-blue Packard with a silver swan hood ornament (or so I thought—eventually I learned that it was a cormorant) drove up late the next afternoon and gave a long blast of the horn at the foot of the veranda steps. The sound echoed up and down the canyon. We were all sitting on the veranda. In one of her rare displays of humor, Mother said, Did I hear something, Scotty? Mr. and Mrs. Nesbitt stepped out of the car talking loudly and cheerfully as if they had only driven a couple of miles up the canyon.

So dramatic, Mrs. Nesbitt shouted up at us, waving her arms at the canyon walls. Why have you kept this so long such a secret?

My god, Alton, I would have never guessed, Mr. Nesbitt seconded. How did you ever find a place like this?

Frank climbed out of the backseat. He was a chubby red-faced kid with short light-brown hair. He looked at me an instant, as if sizing up my gangly frame, and said, Hi, have you got a bike here?

Yeah, I replied.

Let's see it.

There are two.

After Mrs. Nesbitt forced us to *be polite* and say hello to each others' parents, I led him around the back of the lodge to the long wooden shed built up against the cliff next to the garage and pulled open the sagging door. Inside leaning against an old buckboard, one of whose wheels was missing most of its wooden spokes, stood two tall dusty bicycles, a man's and a woman's. Dad and Mother had brought them to the lodge years ago but rarely rode them. I considered them old-fashioned and undignified. The only places they could be ridden were the smoother portions of the dirt road down to Basalt Junction. Most of the road in the canyon was too rocky.

The tires any good?

We squeezed the tires. They were mostly flat.

Got a pump?

A tire pump hung from a nail. I took it down and handed it to him.

I'll take the man's bike, Frank proposed. You get the girl's, okay?

He wheeled the black bike out into the sun and was unscrewing the cap to the rear tube when Mr. Nesbitt strode around the house and shouted, What the hell you think you're doing? Get back there and help your mother unpack the car.

Frank threw down the bike and followed his father around the house. I tagged along, not wanting to pump up the tires. The trunk of the Packard was open. Mr. Nesbitt was setting shiny tan leather suitcases on the ground. Like the car, they were obviously new. Here, get that one upstairs to the guest room, he said to his son, nodding at the largest of the cases. On the double. Then he turned to me. Scotty, you can take this.

Where are you putting Frankie? He was holding out Frank's Boy Scout uniform on a hanger. On the way here they had picked Frank up from summer Scout camp. I recoiled at the thought of touching the faded olive-drab material, because it belonged to *him* and to a lesser degree because I wasn't a Boy Scout. We moved around too much between the lodge, Denver, and occasionally Chicago for me ever to join. He shook it at me. I took it by the metal hook of the hanger so as not to touch the material.

In my room, I guess.

I led the way, holding the uniform away from my body. Behind me Frank dragged the suitcase up the stone steps. Pick up the goddamn thing or else you'll scratch it to pieces, Mr. Nesbitt shouted. We walked through the living room and headed up the staircase, Frank panting behind me. Mrs. Nesbitt was in the guest room poking through a small vanity case, also of tan leather. When Frank dragged in the suitcase she said to no one in particular, I don't know where we're going to put everything. He set it down in the doorway. Just don't leave it there, put it on the bed, she added.

I handed him his uniform and led him next door to my room. Hey, I get the top bunk, he said, throwing the uniform up on my sleeping bag. The thought of him wallowing around up there where Rosalind had so recently slept upset me more than his uniform and its little gold pins and cloth merit badges, but the possibility had dimly occurred to me before that he might make a claim to my bunk. I would stand my ground.

I have asthma, I said. I have to sleep up there. This was not exactly true. When I was much younger I had had a couple of asthma attacks. I didn't think I still had it, though Mother often offered it as an excuse for what she saw as my lethargy. He has asthma, you know. She made a point of alerting everyone to all the illnesses and conditions present, especially hers—at least the socially presentable ones. Dad's good health defied her, but there was always the potential for trouble ahead in the future. He may have his father's bad heart after all, she often confided to women friends. Or, cancer does run in his family, you know. Such remarks caused dinner guests to shift in their chairs.

Frank's darting blue eyes held steady for a moment. They were evenly set in his blocky head, against smooth yet flushed downy skin and his mother's jowly cheeks.

Do you wheeze?

Sometimes.

Better not wheeze when I'm trying to sleep. He snatched up his uniform and threw it on the lower bunk. That's an order.

His father was shouting for him downstairs. We went down and carried the rest of the luggage up. Mother and Dad were in the kitchen laying out pots and pans to begin cooking dinner. Dad rarely went into the kitchen except to see how dinner was progressing. I had a sense that the two of them might be hiding out from the Nesbitts. I couldn't think of any excuse to join them. When Frank and I were done carrying stuff upstairs we went back outside. Mr. Nesbitt was a broad man with a cold blue stare, always watchful, which warmed little even when his lips curled in a smile and he erupted in deep belly laughs. Frankie, remember what I told you, Mr. Nesbitt said and turned away, apparently releasing us to go about our business.

Once we were behind the house, it began. Okay, Alton, pump up those tires. It'll be good for your asthma.

I squatted down and tightened the nozzle on to the valve stem and stood up and began pumping. It was an old tire pump, whose leather gasket was almost worn out or dried up and sometimes it wouldn't pump at all. I stopped and went inside the shed and came back with an oil squirt can, also defective, but managed to get a few drops in the tiny oil hole in the ferrule at the top of the pump. Jesus Christ, gimme that, Frank said, impatient at my slowness, though his more violent pumping accomplished less than mine. Eventually we got the tires pumped up.

Come on, let's go up that road, he said, meaning the road that ran along the tracks before dipping down to end at the lodge. We pushed the bikes up the hill behind the house, a rutted and rocky stretch that was just steep enough to defeat a driver in a heavily loaded car if he didn't keep up his speed in defiance of the roughness of the track. A miscalculation would result in having to back the car down the grade and start all over again. Before leaving for the mine for extended periods, Dad would drive the LaSalle up to the top of the hill and park it in a wide spot in the road; that way Mother wouldn't have to negotiate the steep part if she needed to drive down to Basalt Junction. By the top of the hill Frank was puffing and wheezing, not me.

Okay, Alton, I'll have you a race. First one down gets the top bunk, okay?

With some awkwardness he slung his leg up over the bar of the tall bike and shoved himself away down the hill. I climbed on the girl's bike and followed slowly, tentatively, as he went shooting down the slope, the bike wobbling and then skidding out of control over to the high side of the road, plunging Frank into the branches of a squat juniper. I rolled past him slowly, coaster brake squealing, just far enough past to establish the principle that I was first. I stopped and dismounted.

Goddamn son of a bitch, he shouted as he struggled to free himself from both the bike and the branches, goddamn bike of yours, Alton, goddamn it. Just before landing in the juniper branches the bike had hit a large rock. The front wheel had collapsed and the rim was jammed up against the fork, tire and tube dangling in the air. Frank had gotten in trouble at school for swearing in front of the whole class at the pencil sharpener and had been held after school to write on the blackboard a hundred times, *I will speak courteously at all times*, an embarrassing exercise for someone his age. This had made him late home and no doubt subject to yet more punishment.

He struggled to his feet. His pants were ripped just below the pocket. He pulled the bike out of the branches and then threw it back down. What a lousy bike that is, Alton. He strode away unsteadily down the hill. At one point he stopped and brushed his arm across his eyes as if he might be crying.

I didn't know what to do with the wrecked bike. If I told Dad about how it happened he might say something to Mr. Nesbitt, who would then go after Frank. It would all end with him swearing at me from the bottom bunk—or doing something worse. I leaned my bike against the bank and dragged Frank's the rest of the way down the hill and into the shed, to a far corner where its damaged wheel would not be readily visible in the shadows. Then I walked back and got the blue bike and rode it slowly down the rest of the hill and leaned it against the other, additionally shielding the damage from view.

Frank was nowhere in sight. He must have gone inside the lodge. The sun was approaching the western rim of the canyon.

To go inside would invite questions and scoldings from both sets of parents about Frank's torn and dusty pants and perhaps even some kind of argument, so I climbed up through the rocks behind the shed to my private meadow, where I sat down on a warm slab of basalt. From here I could see the river at the lower end of the beach and the rockslides and cliffs that made up the canyon wall to the west, where the odd twisted piñon tree clung among the boulders.

The presence of the Nesbitts threatened the loose routines of my days. My notions of possession were still circumscribed: my treasures, my clothes, which yet belonged more to Mother than to me because she still picked them out on our fall shopping trips to Denver department stores or once even to Marshall Field's in Chicago, the bike I had to leave back in Denver, the room I had to often share but that was still mine. The lodge was the source of my earliest memories, and I anticipated our summer trips to it with more fervor than any other family activity. "The lodge" encompassed the beach and the river and the canyon and the expanding reaches of my fitful explorations. I didn't see it as "my property" in the truculent playground sense; it was obviously Dad and Mother's, at least above a certain physical stratum that only I inhabited, it seemed, along with the grasses lining the river bank, and up at my meadow, the mosses, the cholla and prickly-pear cacti, the lizards, the late-blooming pink penstemon, the contorted piñon and juniper trees, the boulders in the river, the water boatmen, trout fry I called "minnows" in the still eddies at the edge of the flow, soft brown frogs' eggs adhering to underwater rocks, pollywogs, toads, dragonflies at rest on rocks in the sun, cliff swallows across the river mining dabs of clay for their nests high up in the rocks. Adults didn't possess these things because they moved too unheedingly through the landscape, they didn't notice, they no longer apparently saw, touched, heard. It was as if they were always on their way to somewhere else and were weighed down by memories or visions of Denver or Chicago or wherever else they had come from and about which they spent long hours talking in the living room or out on the veranda. The things here were mine because of my special knowledge of them. Yet I was well aware that adults had some greater power that floated above my world. They could sweep everything away with a wave of the hand. Not Dad or Mother, they wouldn't, because they seemed almost as remote from this larger thing as I was, but people like the Nesbitts, and Mr. Nesbitt in particular, with his thick forearms covered in curly reddish hair.

Without Frank present I would have simply disappeared to my haunts for most of the day, letting the adults go about their business, but with him here I knew I was expected to be the considerate host. Aunt Ruby had once scolded me for having sent Mickey back down the river alone from an afternoon hike—they were leaving after a two-week stay and we wouldn't see them until the end of the summer—while I continued on alone upriver to a favorite pond. The longer I stayed away up at my meadow the more likely I was to be reproached for hiding from Frank when I finally came down. Nonetheless I stayed until the sun touched the ridge.

The bell on the veranda rang out.

I dragged myself down the hill and slipped in through the back door. Mother was fussing over the wood range. Where were you, young man? Would you go find Frank? Dinner's about ready. I think he's in your room.

Dad and the Nesbitts were strolling into the living room from the veranda. Think about it, Scotty. It might work for both of us, Mr. Nesbitt said, patting Dad on the back.

I went upstairs. Frank was sitting on the lower bunk with his suitcase open beside him. He had changed his clothes. There were reddish pouches under his eyes. He looked away when I came in. I told him dinner was almost ready and went back downstairs with my book and slouched down on the couch. The men stood in the dining room while Mrs. Nesbitt carried steaming serving plates from the kitchen and set them down in the center of the table. Everyone sit down, she ordered.

Frank came down the stairs. I slid into my chair at the far end of the table, a space away from where the four adults sat around the other end, with Dad at the head. Frank took his place opposite me. I avoided looking at him. The adults were drinking from brown bottles of Schlitz brought by the Nesbitts, except for Mother, who had a glass of sherry. Mrs. Nesbitt was flushed, the creases between rolls of flesh on her neck marked with lines of perspiration.

This must be such a wonderful place to pass a vacation, she was proclaiming, with the river and all these rocks, so many rocks. I have never seen so many rocks in all my life. How on earth could they ever get here? So many, have you ever seen so many, what do you call them, boulders?

She chattered on. She had a slightly peculiar way of talking, perhaps a trace of an accent though nothing like the suave accents of French people or war-movie Nazis, and her voluble enthusiasm for the trivial stood out from the reticence of my parents, for whom saying much of anything was an effort. Mr. Nesbitt was listening to her with lips clamped shut. Then he interrupted.

So how did your father get this place, Scotties?

My grandfather, Dad corrected. He shifted in his chair, glanced at Mother. Had Aunt Ruby been here she would have jumped in and told the story, concluding with a jovial, And it's been downhill ever since, hasn't it, Scotty? But she wasn't here to come to the rescue. Dad cleared his throat.

My grandfather was connected with the railroad.

Oh the railroads! Mrs. Nesbitt said with a dismissive wave of her hand.

What the hell do you know about the railroads? Mr. Nesbitt shot back.

His grandfather, Mother explained, was an investor in the railroad. He ended up with this section of land. Is that right, Scotty?

A whole section, did he? Mr. Nesbitt nodded his head approvingly.

Several, Mother added, though this is the only one left.

In the family, Dad added.

So you have a whole section here, do you, Scott?

Please explain to me this section business, Mrs. Nesbitt demanded. I do not know what means *section*.

Mr. Nesbitt growled out an explanation of how the government handed out square miles of land to the railroads to encourage them to build new lines. On each side of the tracks, do I have that right, Scott?

Dad was never called *Scott* but Mr. Nesbitt was one of those men who would try out all the variations on your name to see which one makes you the most uncomfortable. By the end of their stay he went through all variations of *Scotty* before moving into *ALL-ten*, *AL-tone*, and plain *Al* for *Alton*. He referred to his wife, Roberta, as *the Missus, the Wife, the Wife and Mistress, Bertha, Berta,* and *Bert*. Only Frank was largely excused from this name torturing, having only to put up with *Frankie* on occasion. And Mother, with whom he was formal and flattering. So far he had ignored me other than to observe randomly, He's so skinny you can see right through him.

Show him, Mother said after a sip of sherry. It's still light out.

Dad got up from the table and led Mr. Nesbitt out to the veranda. Mrs. Nesbitt trailed after them. Her long silky dress displayed only ankles, not calves.

Dad pointed up to the top of the ridge. The southwest corner is up there, near that pointed rock, and the northwest corner is just over the ridge, somewhere in there. You can't see the eastern boundary from here, but it's well above the tracks.

There was a surveying error, Mother called from her place at the table. Frank, would you like seconds?

Yes, please, Mrs. Alton.

Frank had cleaned up his plate despite still looking miserable. The three adults regained the table.

And so what's around it, Scotts?

Forest Service land.

They've been trying to buy the place from us, Mother added.

For how much?

Dad shrugged and looked away. We've never asked, Mother said.

What, do they want more rocks or what? Mrs. Nesbitt said with a mocking curl of her lips.

It's because of the springs along this part of the river, Dad explained. They want the water for campgrounds they're planning for down below the Sluice Box.

Sluice Box? What is this Sluice Box?

Mother described it for Mrs. Nesbitt. The conversation carried on in this vein for the rest of the meal, through dessert, coffee, after-dinner brandy. Frank and I were sent off to the kitchen to wash and dry the dishes. Out of sight of his parents he began coming back to his old self, but he handled the dishes so clumsily that I feared he would break a plate, setting off another cycle of punishment and sulking.

Hey, he said to me as he dried, his large burning presence too close, I betcha I know something you don't.

What?

Shhh, not here. When we go up to your room.

But I stalled. The adults had moved to the living room, the men slouching and smoking in the rustic log armchairs, the women sitting more upright on the couch, Mother at her knitting. I took my book out to the veranda swing where there was just enough light to read from a bare bulb in the center of the ceiling. On a cool breeze there came the first night sounds from the river: crickets, frogs, the splash of a leaping trout, the click of bats fluttering above the cottonwoods. Frank went upstairs without me. Mr. Nesbitt kept up his booming questions about the property and the lodge, now and then backing off into more innocent-seeming queries.

And the fishing, *All-tone*, how is the fishing?

I'm hardly the fisherman my grandfather was.

The mine hasn't helped, I'm sure, Mother added in her absent knitting voice.

And how is that? Mrs. Nesbitt demanded.

Water from the tailing ponds. Sometimes the fall rains turn the river gray. It kills the fish.

How terrible! These ponds, what do you call them, they are next door or where?

Oh no. Twenty miles upstream, Scotty?

More, thirty, thirty-five. It doesn't happen very often, said Dad, smoothing over this unpleasant detail. Once in five years, if that.

The conversation turned away from the lodge to the mine and I lost interest and fell deep into my reading, pleased to leave behind the immediate world around me, a world invaded and now controlled by the Nesbitts, all three of them, for a place where gripping problems and agonies were others', not my own. This was perhaps the first time I willed my reading to displace the real world and in effect willed my own life to become like my reading, so that instead of picking up a book and spreading open the pages at will I could open and close my real life whenever I wanted to and even go for long periods of time without experiencing it at all. I hoped that when I reopened the book of my life I would find the Nesbitts long gone from the lodge, remaining only as a faint distasteful memory.

Mrs. Nesbitt had raised her voice. Hitler wasn't so bad, you know. He built the autobahns and got everybody back to working.

The Missus, Mr. Nesbitt said even louder, the Missus's family, you have to understand, lost everything they owned in the

Hamburg bombings except the shirts on their backs, isn't that right, Berta?

Don't call me Berta, please, I insist. Yes, the same shirts on their backs. Everything burned to ashes. We are so lucky to have what we have.

Back at home in Denver when Mother and Dad had finished thumbing through issues of *LIFE* magazine I had permission to take them to my room and cut out pictures of the last year or so of the war. I was old enough to begin to have an inkling of what they were about. I did this with a big pair of shears I had to return promptly to Mother's desk. I cut around the borders in nice straight lines, but left out the captions, for which I had no use. Nor did I have any plan for these images of death and destruction, except I favored photos of German soldiers alive and dead, and tanks and planes, and their crisp emblems of iron crosses and swastikas. And when I discovered a trove of back issues in the basement from years I was too young to understand what was going on, I spent hours harvesting photos of the Nazis' marches through Austria, Czechoslovakia, Poland, Denmark, Holland and Belgium, France, eastern Europe and Russia, Greece and North Africa. Mussolini and the Italians and the Japanese interested me much less: their uniforms and equipment lacked the showy belligerence of the Germans'. My collecting stopped about the time the first photos of Belsen and Auschwitz and other camps were published in *LIFE*, followed not long after by photos of Hiroshima and Nagasaki. These images fascinated rather than appalled me—that would come later—and were not what stopped my habit. I had simply grown out of cutting out photos. I ended up with a cardboard box filled with images that had come to lose much of their meaning, stripped as they were from their explanatory context. The box sat in my closet for a couple of years. I didn't even remember throwing it out.

The conversation continued. And as for the Jews, I could tell you stories, couldn't I, Horace?

Mr. Nesbitt changed the subject. What time do we have to get up to go to the mine?

Oh the train isn't until midmorning, Dad said.

Please do excuse me, Mother murmured, but I simply must go to bed. It has been a long day.

I was interested to note that she didn't claim a migraine coming on.

But can't we drive?

Dad described the condition of the road and the route, which was more circular than the rail line. Mr. Nesbitt was confident the Packard would make it. They decided to leave early in the morning. They would be gone perhaps two days. My heart sank. I sensed that it would be futile to be taken along, and if I went then Frank would want to go, too. The men chatted on another half hour about other mines near ours, now the smallest on that stretch of the range, and the geology of the area, Dad reticent to explain what he knew, Mr. Nesbitt quick to follow with more questions.

So this geologist friend of yours, Slater—

Slatter, Dad corrected.

So this Slatter friend of yours, how much longer does he think the area will produce at the present rate, that's what I need to know, Scotts.

He's checking his files at the university. They may tell us.

Tell us or give us an idea?

Mrs. Nesbitt announced she was going to bed, and as soon as I heard her heavy footsteps reach the top of the stairs and clomp down the hall to the guest room, I slipped through the living room and up the stairs and into the bathroom, where I peed. In my room Frank was lying in the upper bunk flipping through some Superman comics.

Get off my bed, I said, surprised at the sharpness of my tone.

Okay, as long as you don't wheeze.

He had already put his pajamas on. He climbed ponderously down the ladder at the end of the bunk, causing the structure to wobble and creak. His Boy Scout uniform hung from one of the steel mattress straps above his pillow. I took my pajamas off the hook behind the door and took them up the ladder and changed in bed, out of his sight. The sleeping bag was warm, almost hot, from his presence. It felt like his body was pressing close to mine. I wondered what position I could assume to minimize my touching the sleeping bag until it cooled down. He got up and turned out the light and crashed back into the lower bunk, giving the upper a sharp lurch.

He asked in the dark, Where did you go?

Nowhere.

After a long silence, he said, Oh, I know where.

I tried to ignore him. I tried to pretend I was reading but of course I had nothing to read in the dark.

You went to get your papers.

What papers? I mumbled as if from near sleep.

But maybe you don't have them yet, maybe they haven't given them to you yet.

What papers?

Your masturbation papers, he hissed, then giggled.

This was the first time I had heard the word. I had no idea what it meant but from his tone I knew it was something dirty. Nor did I have any idea how to reply. *Yes* would mean I knew what he was talking about and therefore might be called on to explain.

No, I said after a long pause.

They're real important, Alton. You're supposed to have them on you at all times.

With Cousin Mickey I might have tried to banter with him to find out what the word meant, to find out whether he really knew or was just pretending to, but not with Frank. He badgered me some more, but with increasing listlessness at my lack of response.

Tangled in the coils of incomprehension, I fell asleep.

I awoke conscious of Frank's presence in the lower bunk and anxious about my ruby. He was snoring lightly. My ruby was hidden behind a loose knot in the pine paneling just above the shelf next to my pillow. I wondered whether I could pry out the knot with my little fingernail to make certain my treasure was still there without making a noise that might alert him. At school Frank filched small objects from other students, a favorite pencil, a lucky charm, and would run and drop or push them between the cracks of the boardwalk that connected the six classrooms of the elementary school. The school was built during the war, and the boardwalk was laid out with large gaps between the boards in order to save scarce lumber. Then he'd try to retrieve the stolen goods through the half-inch cracks with two long pencils or a length of straightened coat hanger. Once an object slipped or was dropped between the cracks it passed into the magical realm of "finders, keepers." Since Frank knew exactly where some of them were, in theory he had a better chance than most at retrieving them, but he was little more successful than the rest of us who spent at least part of each lunch hour staring down in wonderment through the sunlit cracks of the boardwalk, at a seabed littered with sunken treasures so tantalizingly within reach: milk money in the form of pennies, nickels, dimes, even quarters; dozens of pencils; the very first ballpoint pen any of us had ever seen; a few box-top Captain Midnight rings; marbles, particularly peewees; a penknife—or rather, the faint shapes of these objects, which were quickly coated with dust and pellets of mud scraped off shoes during wet weather. Teachers were fitful in discouraging us from crouching in a circle or lying on our stomachs and "fishing" for lost objects with pencils and rulers. Mr. Westin, the sixth-grade teacher, would often call out as he passed by, Now tell me, boys, are we laying on our stomachs or are we lying on them? In either case we're getting our clothes dirty, aren't we? It was too risky to bring a cumbersome flashlight with expensive batteries to school; and Frank himself was briefly suspended for lighting matches and dropping them through the cracks to illuminate the dusty gloom. This had the side effect of curing him of his thieving. The rest of us lost interest in fishing for a while. During the last months of the school year few objects were lost or deliberately pushed down the cracks. When the school was remodeled ten years after the war and the boardwalk torn up to be replaced by a concrete walkway, I imagined the construction workers raking through the detritus of our childhood with little cries of, Hey, look at this, I'll be damned.

I decided against pulling out the knothole plug and risking making a noise. I slipped into my clothes and climbed down the ladder at the foot of the bed, leaving my bedding and pajamas all rumpled up in order to discourage Frank from reclaiming the space during the day. It was impossible to climb up or down the ladder without rocking the whole bed, but Frank slept through my movements, his copy of the thick *Boy Scout Handbook* pushed up against the wall, his uniform swinging back and forth just beyond his pillow like the ghostly presence of a third person. The stuffy animal odor of the room followed me for a short distance into the airy hallway. Footsteps from inside the guest room suggested that the Nesbitts were about to emerge. I skipped down the stairs and across the living room and went out the front door through the veranda, opening and closing it quietly, so as not to alert Dad or Mother, who were banging around in the kitchen.

The midnight-blue Packard, covered in dust, was parked at the bottom of the stone steps. It was the only thing about the Nesbitts I liked. Dad was against buying any of the new postwar cars because he had heard too many stories about lemons, and our 1940 LaSalle still wasn't using much oil. I walked down the steps and sat on the rear bumper and ran my fingers over the passenger-side taillight, the dark raspberry-red glass, the rectangular chrome bezel that made the light look like a giant equal sign. In Denver and Chicago during night drives, I would perch in the middle in the backseat of our car, elbows propped on the back of the front seat, and let the dazzling headlights of cars and dimmer cyclops beams of streetcars wash over my eyes, awaiting darker moments when I could decode the dim red taillights and orange running lights and the faint glow illuminating rear license plates, as if they were exotic night-flying insects, and attach them to brands of cars and trucks and buses and types of streetcars. With delicate strokes I removed the dust from the Packard taillight in a way that wouldn't be easily noticed. It would have been too familiar or daring to sit on the front bumper and clean off the classic chrome grill or the winged cormorant hood ornament, though I wanted to. There was something brooding and important about the car, dark and private, compared to our leaner and more athletic LaSalle with its practical tan paint, the metal of the rear fenders wavy where they had been repaired repeatedly from the effects of Mother's ineptness at backing up.

The sun was warming the blue-painted metal. Sparks shot up out of the kitchen chimney: Dad was firing up the range. The smell of bacon would soon cut through the cool fresh scent of evergreens that rolled down the canyon on quiet mornings, on a barely perceptible breeze. Foolishly I thought that I might be able to figure out something to do with Frank that would be different from our schoolyard encounters—or rather my evasions. But what? He had already wrecked one of the bikes. Whatever those *papers* were, I didn't expect them to help.

You're up, Mother observed from the veranda screen door. Could you please finish setting the table?

Mr. and Mrs. Nesbitt were coming down the stairs when I went back inside the lodge.

Well, Mr. Scotsman Junior, what are you two going to do today when I go up to the mine with Mr. Scotsman Senior, huh? Mr. Nesbitt said with a widemouthed smile, though his blue eyes were slightly narrowed. Mrs. Nesbitt brushed past him and pushed through the swinging kitchen door. You going to keep yourself and my Frankie, he continued, out of trouble for a change? How many fish have you caught this morning?

None.

He came close to me, bent his head down confidentially, swung out an arm to grasp the top of a chair, to corral me. I wish my Frankie were as grown-up as you are, young Scotsman. I don't care how many merit badges he's got, he's still—well . . .

Mrs. Nesbitt swung through the door carrying a platter of toast covered with a linen napkin. Isn't he up yet?

To my relief, Mr. Nesbitt stepped away. He walked over to the foot of the stairs and shouted, Up you get, Frankie, rise and shine. And remember what I told you, dammit.

Horace, please, Mrs. Nesbitt implored before returning to the kitchen.

Filthy habit, son, just remember it's a filthy habit, he said to me in a low voice.

I had no idea what he was talking about, still grappling as I was with the implications of the term *habit*. My ears were especially sensitive to phrases like *He's in the habit of . . .*, which Aunt Ruby applied to Walter with daily frequency, as in *He's in the habit of throwing the newspaper on the floor after reading it as if we have an army of servants to pick it all up afterward*, or *Walter is in the habit of eating up half the hors d'oeuvres before the guests arrive*. In Aunt Ruby's view, Walter was little more than a collection of habits, which were implicitly bad. Mr. Nesbitt's use of the term *filthy* to describe a habit was the first time I had heard or at least paid attention to the combination, and I strained to imagine what that might be. A moment later Frank clomped down the stairs, face red, hair uncombed, tucking his shirt in as he descended, clearly suspect in the practice of some *filthy habit*. By then Mother and Dad had carried the rest of the breakfast out from the kitchen and had spread out the platters on the dining room table and were urging everyone to sit down and begin serving themselves.

Did you wash your hands? Mrs. Nesbitt asked Frank but then turned away without waiting for an answer. Why don't you take the boys up to the mine with you, Horace? I'm sure they want to go.

I don't like it up there, I blurted out, surprised at myself. It's bad for my asthma.

Both Dad and Mother raised their eyes with quizzical looks at each other.

He has asthma in the chest? Mrs. Nesbitt asked, pointing her fork at me.

Where else would he have it, Roberta? Mr. Nesbitt bellowed with a mocking laugh. In the shins?

Childhood asthma, the doctor says, Mother said before taking a mouthful of scrambled eggs, which excused her from elaborating. Eventually she added, There's no place for the boys when the men go below ground, you see. Oh, I forgot the Nucoa.

When margarine began appearing in the stores in butter-yellow squares wrapped in foil just after the end of the war, I had lost the job of kneading the one-pound clear plastic pouches of white margarine in such a way as to break the little packet of orange food coloring within and distribute it evenly through the substance, tinting it yellow.

Mother got up to go to the kitchen. Dad, head bent to eat,

surveyed the scene with wary upturned glances. Frank had heaped his plate with scrambled eggs and bacon. Mr. Nesbitt was fixing him with a steely gaze.

But what is the life of these mines? Mrs. Nesbitt asked. Ten years, twenty years, what?

Mother brought the pale-yellow section of margarine in a butter dish on the table and sat down. This one, she said, has been in the family since—when, Scotty?

Eighteen seventy-nine. They thought it was played out in 1927 and then again ten years later but actually since then we've extracted more silver than in the previous fifty or sixty years. Plus some rare earths during the war years.

You don't say.

But the geology is very complex up there, Dad said. I'm waiting for word from a geologist friend. He paused as if to say more but fell silent.

So there could be nothing left in a year or two, is that what you're saying? Mrs. Nesbitt asked.

Mr. Nesbitt tried to smooth this over. Or fifty or sixty. That's what Scott here is trying to say, Roberta. You don't know. Nobody knows.

She turned to him. We have this saying where I come from, *If nobody knows then everybody knows except you.* That is what you call a good investment, Horace? Are you missing some marbles this morning, or what?

The price of metals goes up enough, you make your money back in a year.

And if it goes down? Kaput?

I'm in the metals business. I know my metals. They're going up. And up and up. That's why we're here.

I won't tell you how much money he wants to invest in chinchillas, Mrs. Nesbitt said, fixing Mother with an indignant stare.

Chinchillas?

Mr. Nesbitt attempted to wrench the conversation back to a more comfortable path. All right, Mr. Scotsman Senior, when are we getting out of this place? Can you be ready in fifteen minutes?

They are nothing but overpriced rabbits, Mrs. Nesbitt threw out in Mother's direction. Overpriced rabbits.

Oh, said Mother. The morning train is due at ten thirty.

Rabbits, just rabbits! Though because of their fancy fur coats they need to be kept in expensive refrigerated, what do you call them, huts?

Hutches?

Refrigerated hutches!

No, no, no, we'll drive, huh, Scotty? That Packard I've got can get up any hill, I tell you. She's just like a jackrabbit, isn't she, Bertha? A real jackrabbit.

Frank made a weak plea to come along but was rebuffed by Mr. Nesbitt. Mrs. Nesbitt remained in a pout the rest of breakfast, her head thrown back defiantly. Mother stared into space, sipping her coffee, probably wondering how she was going to get through the rest of the day.

Just as he was about to push his chair back, Mr. Nesbitt's face became flushed. He looked up and shook his fork at his wife across the table, launching a fragment of scrambled egg up in an arc that ended on the linen napkin folded over the last pieces of toast.

Just you remember, he growled, we did not go one day, one

single day during the war without meat, during the entire war, not one day. Then, perhaps realizing that he might have carried a private dispute with his wife too far, he recomposed his expression into a smile and turned to Dad. All right, Mr. Scotsman Senior, are we ready to get out of this place? Fifteen minutes?

The yellow scrap of egg, no larger than a nail clipping, lay on the napkin. I stared at it, wondering what to do. The adults appeared oblivious to it. Dad was looking at his pocket watch. Mother stood up and moved around the table refilling coffee cups. Frank was inserting a strip of bacon into his mouth and nibbling at it in tiny bites. Mrs. Nesbitt pushed away her plate and pulled her leather purse up onto her lap and began rummaging through it.

I dreaded being drafted to wash and dry the breakfast dishes with Frank, so I was relieved when Mother said she and Mrs. Nesbitt would fix lunches for the men and clean up the kitchen, but my heart sank when she suggested with strained cheerfulness, You boys can go play. I put off the moment by hanging around the Packard while the two men inspected the engine compartment and filled a couple of canvas Desert Water Bags to hang from the front bumper. Frank cleaned out comic books he had left on the backseat and, when his father wasn't looking, a candy bar and a packet of bubble gum from under the front seat. When the women came down the steps with sack lunches and thermoses, Mr. Nesbitt started the engine, a straight-eight that ran rough for a few minutes before smoothing out into a hearty purring. Mother touched Dad on the elbow as a parting gesture and urged him to be careful down in the mine. Mrs. Nesbitt stood back, arms folded, surveying her big man and his big car with pride, her face nonetheless twisted up in a grimace of hurt and anger. Mr. Nesbitt slammed the door, turned his head, and winked at her. Frank sidled up to his mother and whined into her plump elbow, Why can't I go? The car roared off and circled around behind the lodge and up the steep hill to the sound of tires skidding and the ping of gravel hitting the exhaust and frame.

I'll meet you down at the beach, I said to Frank. I have to go to the bathroom first.

Where's the beach?

I pointed through the cottonwoods toward the river. Then I raced up the veranda steps and ran through the living room past the women and up the stairs. After that I took my time. I could go hide, I thought, or bury myself in my book Rosalind-style and pretend I forgot, take refuge in my infinitely more fascinating solitary world. But I wasn't certain whether such techniques would work on Frank. Though subdued and sullen this morning, I knew he could be unpredictable. I went back downstairs, but this time with my more habitual quietness. I knew how to move through the lodge almost silently, adding little to its perpetually creaking responses to heat and cold and wind and changes in humidity, how to avoid the loose floorboard on the lower step and how to walk close to the wooden partition walls so as to put less strain on noisy floor joists, and I could even soundlessly open and close the easily rattled thumb latches on the plank doors. Decades later while visiting a museum that had once been a warlord's palace outside of Tokyo, I was intrigued to discover that the flooring of the hallways had been deliberately constructed to squeak in key places, to alert the guards of suspicious movements during the night. Mother was never entirely aware of the fact that usually she didn't know where I was because of my quiet movements, and most of the time she imagined me where in fact I was no longer—back up in my room, for example, not sitting in the dining room within earshot of conversations the adults were having over coffee in the kitchen. This is where I often overheard Aunt Ruby unburden herself of her more interesting assertions while the two women reluctantly worked together in the kitchen. Mother was a fretful, unimaginative cook, always insecure about the results, while Aunt Ruby, who had been to France before the war and who had become minimalist well before it was fashionable, stood by in exasperation as everything was either *overcooked* or *over-gravied*. For her part Mother was captive in her own kitchen to the unspoken rule that women guests, especially relatives, had to help out but could not take over. It was there that Aunt Ruby occasionally needled Mother to urge Dad to sell the mine before it was too late, without explaining what she meant by that. On an earlier visit she had said while they were both standing at the sink, with an irritable edge to her voice, Everyone who would care is long dead: Father, Grandfather, Scotty's and my great-grandfather. And Scotty Junior is not going to have anything to do with it, I'm sure. Mother's brief reply had been inaudible.

Now as I slipped into a chair and opened *The Way of All Flesh* to my page, Mother was at the sink, with Mrs. Nesbitt drying dishes at her side. We almost had to take him, Mrs. Nesbitt said, early from summer Scout camp.

Mrs. Nesbitt was incapable of speaking softly, while Mother was equally incapable of raising her voice. But this time I was fairly certain I heard Mother say, Perhaps Frank should have his own room.

No, we have told him he must put on his best behavior.

There was a long silence. I sensed that I had overheard confidences which might lead to complications should it be discovered that I was in on them, but at the same time I had no idea what it was all about, other than there was another aspect of Frank's character I had to watch out for beyond his tendency to bully. This seemed yet another reason to delay meeting him at the beach. I eased away from the table silently and glided through the veranda and squeezed though the screen door, which squeaked and sang only if you pushed it all the way open, and slowly closed it after me. At the bottom of the stone steps I turned left and followed the veranda to the end, where I ducked down and unlatched the square hatch, a wood frame covered with wire mesh, into the basement underneath the lodge. Legs first, I inserted myself inside the darkness. The basement was in fact no more than a crawl space, except someone had dug trenches leading deep under the house. I could walk in them hunched over or else slide along on my knees without banging my head on the joists. The space served to store household goods no longer needed and on the way to being thrown away. Just inside the hatchway a string ran halfway across the space to the pull chain of a light fixture. I gave it a tug. The light went on. The slightly humid air smelled of mold.

Nothing had changed since my last visit the summer before. Near the hatchway sat several wooden boxes filled with Dad's old mining magazines, mainly *The American Mining Engineer* and *The World Mining Journal*. Occasionally I flipped through more current issues upstairs or in the Denver house but I found the gray photos of mining equipment and pumps and tunnels boring and at times even menacing. Dad never tried to interest me in them. The wooden boxes with dovetailed corners were another matter: lettered in red and black they read *TROJAN EXPLOSIVES*. Dad had brought them down from the mine. One day I would find a use for the boxes, empty the magazines into something else. A sagging cardboard carton contained tarnished Victorian urns and pitchers of apparently no practical use and a grocery bag of scratched 78 records which I had gone through several times in search of interesting titles to play on the windup Victrola in a dark corner of the living room, a machine that would have been relegated to the crawl space itself had it fit through the hatch. *Horses Don't Bet on People, They Have Too Much Horse Sense* was the only record I had moved from the basement to a trunk under my bunk bed. Other records gathered dust in the lower cabinet of the Victrola, including *Treasure Island*, which I had outgrown except for the hoarse gargling scream of a pirate being stabbed and which now and then I still liked to play over and over again. There were other cartons of stove pots without handles, which had somehow missed being contributed to the scrap-metal drives during the war, canning jars, tin cans, unmatched silver plate, parts of lamps, radio tubes. A black widow, the same I had seen last year, or one of her descendants, nested between a joist and a floorboard directly above the hatch. I regretted not having brought down a flashlight to illuminate more clearly her black form next to the white nest ball.

I usually came down here when I felt I might find something

new in the boxes, but it all seemed drably familiar this time, and I knew I wouldn't be able to stay down here long. I switched out the light and was about to crawl back outside when I heard footsteps on the stone stairs and then across the boards of the veranda above my head. Frank had returned from the beach. I squeezed out through the hatch and headed down through the cottonwoods to the river, hoping to be out of sight by the time he had searched through the house. The water was still running milky tan from the recent flood. Bands of reddish clay along the beach were drying and cracking into small pieces and curling up in the sun. It seemed it had been weeks since Rosalind had left, not just a few days. I imagined her curled up in a corner of the backseat of the Studebaker, reading her way across the Mojave Desert. The windows would be open in the heat. Now and then they'd stop for gas. Before anyone else, Rosalind would jump out of the car and run inside and quickly buy a postcard and a stamp and then go hide in a stall in the women's room, scribble me a card. *Dear Scotty*, she'd write, *I don't know what to say and I have to go now. We're in something-Tree . . . Rosalind.* She'd slip the postcard to the clerk while Mr. Slatter was still filling up the gas tank. But there the reverie ended, with the realization that the Rosalind I actually knew was not quick and clever in this way She'd still be reading.

I had outgrown the business of making roads in the sand and building suburbs of mill-end houses surrounded by plantings of evergreen twigs, but I could sit on the sand where it was drying and warming in the sun, my back against a boulder, and restructure the space around me as a miniature landscape entwined with roadways and punctured with sticks for telephone poles connected by invisible wires, all the while keeping an eye on the flowing water for an irregular swirl on the surface in the near distance and staying alert for a fluttering wing in the willows on the other side of the river. It must have come to me very young, this ability to sit outside in some favorite place and remain immobile for extended periods of time, becoming aware of the traffic of ants and spiders on the ground nearby, flies, gnats, the changes of light and shadow with the passage of time, the elusive forming and dissolving patterns in water, even the way the air moved during ostensibly still moments, and the approach and distancing of birdcalls, the swallows skimming just above the surface, and the pulsations of the sound of flowing water that came with breezes and gusts of wind. Up until this time in my life I was in some sense bodiless, or my body was able to register only the grossest sensations, the initial sting of cold water when I went wading, the hot sand in the heat of the afternoon, and not the subtle gradations between extremes. Now for perhaps the first time I felt the softness of the fine sand beneath my palms, the nubby surface of the boulder pressing against my back, the sun falling on my hair and ears and neck, a trickle of perspiration working its way down my ribs beneath the material of my shirt, sensations I had surely always known but never quite so consciously heeded. Later I would begin to connect this sensual unfolding, or leafing out, which in a sense was never entirely to stop, with my reading or with that dreamy state with which I ran my eyes over certain passages in novels, when my imagination picked up cues and spun them into elaborate shapes and sounds and sensations that probably had little to do with the actual texts, either because I was still too inexperienced to understand what these passages were describing or because I was as yet untrained in harnessing my thoughts to the words and images before my eyes. I was not yet reading whole books, even though I turned every page and my eyes took in every word. I was reading only about a third or less, my mind filling in the rest.

I was so deep into taking in the details of my little corner of the beach that Frank's approach from behind came as a rude shock. I hadn't heard him coming through the cottonwoods.

Hey, where have you been, Scotty? Here let me show you how to do a hammerlock.

Before I knew it he had bounded across the sand and dropped to his knees and wrapped an arm around my neck, twisting my right arm back and trying to throw me down on the sand.

This is what they do to scouts who don't have their masturbation papers, he gasped, his hot breath on my neck.

I tried to elbow him with my free left arm but only managed to graze his soft stomach. He was hurting my arm. I grunted. Show me yours, I squeezed out while trying to free myself.

Abruptly he let go and stood up and brushed the sand off his pants and tucked his shirt back in and then shuffled over to some rocks embedded in the sand and clay. He bent over and dug one out with his fingers, hoisted it up, and heaved it into the water. It hit with a broad splash followed by a *clunk* as it hit the rocks just below the surface.

Come on, Scotty, let's see who can throw the biggest farthest.

Go ahead.

What?

Go ahead, I shouted.

Frank walked up and down the sand and through the band of clay in search of anything he could throw into the water, sticks, small logs, rocks he could barely lift, small stones that he ricocheted off the boulders far out in the water or else tried to skip along the surface. Since much of what he picked up was smeared with clay, still damp on the underside, his pants ended up daubed and streaked with the reddish-tan substance. I sat, trying to lose myself in my own thoughts and figure out how to slip away without his noticing. The once-quiet morning air was wracked with splashing explosions and Frank's triumphant cries. Hey, watch this one. Boy, that was a good one. Watch out, that one's really going to splash. After launching a particularly large rock, he stumbled into the water, soaking his shoes. At last he stopped. He sat down on a boulder, pulled off his shoes and socks, baring his white feet. His jowly face was red from exertion.

My father is going to buy this place, you know.

No, he's not, I shot back, pierced by a pang of uncertainty.

Oh yes he is. He told me.

When?

On the way here. The mine, too. He's going to buy the mine, too.

I said nothing. The mine had been a source of family anxiety as long as I could remember. But the lodge? I had come to anticipate our summers at the lodge with a keenness that in retrospect perhaps helped the adults put up with the quiet and isolation. Scotty Junior loves it here, I could often hear Mother saying, perhaps masking her own feelings. Then, this past year, perhaps even earlier this summer, I had finally grasped that she really didn't like spending summers here but did so because

Dad insisted and, I suppose, to please me. I had not yet extended her distaste for summers at the lodge to the thought of its eventual sale. This suddenly seemed obvious. Her dislike would win out. The lodge would be sold.

Race you back to the house, I yelled, jumping to my feet and speeding off through the trees, knowing that Frank would be unable to keep up, exhausted and shoeless from his noisy efforts. I dashed up the front steps and through the veranda, where Mother and Mrs. Nesbitt were knitting, and through the house and quietly out the back door and started to head up the hillside to my private meadow when I realized I could hold out up there longer if I had my book. I darted back through the kitchen, which smelled of bacon. The bound volume was still on the dining room table.

Scotty, Mother called out from the veranda, was there any mail?

What?

Didn't you meet the train this morning?

No, I forgot.

I was stung. Frank's antics down at the river and then his claim that Mr. Nesbitt was going to buy the lodge had so distracted me that I had failed to pay attention to the train laboring up the grade—though now I could remember it clearly clanking its way past, with Frank pausing only briefly in his messy labors to watch it.

I'll go this afternoon, I called out before resuming my way out the back door. There was a corner of my meadow shaded by an old juniper. I threw myself down on the ground and caught my breath. The rain had added a distinct lushness to the apron of grass fed by the water-tank seepage. The meadow was situated at about the level of the roof of the lodge, and an uneven row of boulders masked me from view from below, and the path up to the larger spring that fed the water tank was screened by more boulders and the juniper. It was my most reliable hiding place. No one had ever found me here.

I wished Aunt Ruby were here to make the Nesbitts as uncomfortable as Frank was making me. She could put him in his place. What are you feeding that young man, she would say to Mrs. Nesbitt, as she once said to another, gasoline? I've always thought that rudeness was a particularly ugly disease, don't you agree? A few more remarks of that tone usually effected changes in behavior or else departures from the house earlier than planned. Mother was too polite to do more than furrow her brow and suggest some kind of board game, Monopoly or Parcheesi, or a card game, which she believed would cause everyone to settle down and become proper little gentlemen and ladies.

I opened my book and read. The rest of the morning drifted by. Occasionally I would look up and watch a robin drinking from a puddle near the spring. A fat golden-mantled squirrel regularly checked on my presence from its burrow on the far side of the spring, darting in and out of sight, small tail held high. A red dragonfly buzzed by the site every now and then. Younger, I had been obsessed with trying to catch the creatures, fast-flying and seemingly purposeful, whose Piper Cub–like form I found elegant, but I had never succeeded and was now resigned to simply watching them come and go and occasionally land near the water and perch on a clump of cattails, four horizontal iridescent wings held immobile, bulbous eyes soaking up the world. A few sounds came from the lodge below, the

slamming of the front and back screen doors, Frank occasionally calling out my name in an irritated voice, upstairs windows
opening and closing.

I couldn't entirely conceive of the lodge being *sold*. It
meant, I knew, that we could probably no longer come here,
but what about our belongings? Where would they go? Or
would Mr. Nesbitt keep it exactly as it was? Dad and Mother
resisted changing much of anything. I don't see why you insist
on keeping this place like a shrine to Grandfather, Ruby had
once blurted out over drinks before dinner. Look at those
cobwebs up there! They must be mid-Victorian at least!
Mother had suggested there was nothing in the lodge long
enough to reach up to the far corners of the high-beamed ceiling. I'll bring something from Denver next time, Ruby had
retorted. Unless you want to preserve them for posterity.

Nor did I know exactly how to form questions to Mother
about the possible sale. I sensed that it was one of those things
I would not be invited to think about beforehand: I would be
told when it was all over.

The veranda bell summoned me to lunch. I slipped in
through the back door. Mother was alone in the kitchen. How
long are they going to be here? I whispered. But Mrs. Nesbitt
pushed through the swinging door from the dining room, raised
her plucked eyebrows.

Where have you been? Frank has been looking all places for
you.

I was reading, I muttered.

Oh, she whooped with a sarcastic tone. Oh!

Frank was in the dining room eating his sandwich. Where
have you been?

Reading, I said archly, as if that was the best way to pass the morning, which everyone ought to know.

Mrs. Nesbitt carried the rest of sandwiches in. Frank, how many times have I said to you not to eat until everyone sits themselves down, don't you hear?

So lunch passed, with Mrs. Nesbitt enjoining Frank to sit up straight, use his napkin, not leave the crusts, and Mother asking me not to read at the table. When I finished first and stood up, she cast a quizzical look at me but didn't stop me from leaving the room. I heard her explain, He likes to be alone sometimes, as if it were a personality trait and not a way to flee a disliked playmate. I slipped out through the kitchen screen door and retreated back up the hill.

When the train whistle sounded midafternoon from the top of the grade, I felt released from my meadow retreat, in which I was feeling imprisoned by my own stubbornness. I had begun to restore my morale by thinking I could somehow get the better of Frank and bully him right back and into some kind of submission. After waiting long enough, I hoped, for the train to make its way most of the way down the grade, I scrambled up the rocks and joined the switchback path up the hill. When the train rounded the corner, it was longer and slower than usual, with two engines this time. The engineer gave a quick toot when he saw me. From the baggage car at the end, Mr. Sanchez peered out, then disappeared for a moment, reemerged, and gracefully leaned out and handed me two letters and a telegram in a yellow envelope and a post-office slip announcing that there was a Special Delivery parcel waiting to be picked up.

Would you tell your mother that Mrs. Smedley wouldn't

give me the package? he called back as the train rocked and squealed slowly away downhill.

This would mean a trip by car down to Basalt Junction the next day. I always looked forward to these, even when Mother drove, and now even with the prospect of having to sit in the backseat with Frank. I skipped and jumped down the steep hill, from rock to rock, with an expertness born of frequent practice. Two-thirds of the way down, I passed Frank laboring up a steep section of the path that had worn steplike incisions in the slope. He was on all fours, face red, shirt untucked again.

Hi, I said as I danced down past him.

Mother wanted to leave early in the morning for Basalt Junction in order to get back before the afternoon thunderstorms usually started. Not thinking he would be away that long, Dad hadn't parked the LaSalle at the top of the hill in order to spare Mother the ordeal of negotiating the steep ascent herself. I was both nervous and excited. I had avoided Frank much of the day before, and as a result he had become subdued and sullen. I read all evening in the living room while he thumbed irritably through the same comic books over and over again, ignoring suggestions from his mother. Go inside that book room and find a good book to look at, she said again and again. No, he replied, there's nothing in there. Now and then he would tramp up the stairs to my room and return after a while with another set of already-read comic books. When I finally went to bed I could tell from the arrangement of my sleeping bag and pillow that he had climbed up there and wallowed around, but I pretended not to notice the desecration.

Mother backed the LaSalle out of the garage after breakfast. Mrs. Nesbitt settled herself into the front seat, Frank and I got in the back, me sitting behind Mother. I flipped the center armrest down sharply as if to say I wanted no nonsense from him. Mother had prepared sack lunches for everyone, with the idea that we might stop by the river somewhere on the way back. There was something special about these rare vacation lunch bags, little bundles of sandwiches and cookies wrapped in waxed paper, sometimes an apple or a banana, and after the war, a little square of Hershey's chocolate drawn from one of Mother's expert hiding places—expert in the sense that I was never able to find them. The packets were stacked in inverse order of eating, bologna sandwich at the bottom, chocolate at the top, in a brown paper bag neatly folded over to close—and always, somehow, even out at the lodge, a brand-new paper bag, not a used one. I carried these little artificial stomachs, which is how I thought of them, around very carefully so as not to disturb the layered order of the contents; and when the moment came to sit down and unfold the top of the bag and reach down inside for the sandwich, always cut in four like at a fancy reception, it was often the most memorable event of the day. To protect my lunch bag, I slipped it into the space between my feet and the door, as far out of Frank's reach as possible. I could too easily imagine him setting off some tussle that would end with ripped paper sacks and contents spilled all over the backseat.

Mother directed the long nose of the car up the steep, rutted hill.

Do you think we can go up this? Mrs. Nesbitt asked, clutching the sill of the open window.

The only time Mother wore glasses was when she drove, and I could sense her eyes shifting back and forth at the unfamiliar clarity of the view, the protruding rocks, the deep ruts. Though I hadn't learned to drive yet I knew from watching Dad that she was using the clutch too much and not giving it enough gas. She would stall the engine halfway up and have to back down and start all over again. I pulled myself forward with the lap robe cord, deepened my voice.

Give it more gas, Mother. And get your foot off the clutch.

She gave it too much gas. Barely under her control the car veered right and left up the hill and lurched in and out of ruts and bounced over rocks, rear wheels skidding, to the sound of rattling doors and squeaking seat springs, gravel showering down the slope. The glove-box door flew open. At the top, she stopped for no apparent reason, let out a deep sigh, and then resumed, crossing the railroad tracks. For the rest of the way down the canyon the road paralleled the tracks and was rough and slow but not steep, and the trick was not to be fooled by one of the smooth stretches into speeding up too much and hitting the next rough stretch too fast. Dad keeps it in first gear all the way through here, I coached from the backseat.

Frank seemed unusually quiet and still. I was content to examine through the open window the basalt boulders on the steep slope to our left as we wallowed past them at little more than a walking pace, wondering which of the huge jagged lumps might be likely to roll down on to the roadway or the railroad tracks in the next big storm. Blue-green sage and rabbit bush grew in clumps among them and, more sparsely, piñon and juniper trees, darker and denser in foliage, among which flitted the blur of an occasional bird, towhee or junco or Townsend's solitaire or chickadee or robin. Higher above, the slope became a sheer cliff of long cracks and blocklike boulders stacked precariously on top of each other. I entertained myself with visions of apocalyptic rockslides following our passage. After about five miles the road emerged from the mouth of the canyon just past the site of a future Forest Service campground and became smoother and wider, a sandy swath across a flatter expanse of sage with only a few rough patches through shallow gullies. The trick here, I knew, was to drive relatively fast while anticipating where you had to slow down and by how much, which I also knew that Mother did not entirely grasp. Leaning forward, I kept on coaching her from the backseat.

At one point out of the corner of my eye I noticed Frank pull something out of his right front pants pocket with some difficulty. Whatever it was, he held it cupped before him in his two hands, opening and closing them to peek at it. I sat back and turned to look. I was pierced by a sense of despair—and then anger. My ruby, my treasure. Stolen!

Face burning, I turned away. Too late I felt Mother slam on the brakes before we went clattering and bouncing through a gully. On smooth ground again, the car still ran, nothing banging. You didn't warn me, Scotty, she said, raising her eyes to the rearview mirror. I leaned forward and tried to pay attention to the road. Mrs. Nesbitt stared straight ahead, her jaw set, right hand gripping the vent-window post.

Frank must have somehow dislodged the hiding-place knot while up in my bunk. I had not thought to check it recently.

Slow down just past that tree, I said to Mother.

How could I get it back? I wasn't strong enough to over-power him and was affronted at the thought of whining to Mother that Frank had stolen my ruby. She wouldn't know what I was talking about. A ruby? A real ruby? I would have to explain. Oh that, she'd say. The only thing I could do would be to somehow maneuver Frank into a position where he'd have to give it back without the intervention of the adults. But how?

It's okay along here for about a mile, I think, I said.

I rolled the window the rest of the way down and let the warm air flow over me. As we glided through this rolling plain of tree stumps and scrub growth left over from logging, with a line of gray peaks to the west, a stretch whose openness I normally enjoyed after the confinement of the canyon, I felt flushed and anxious at this new problem thrust on me by Frank. I was unable to fix on anything except vaguely the gently wind-ing roadway ahead and was barely able to remember the next bad patch I needed to alert Mother to. Mrs. Nesbitt had de-cided to relieve her own anxieties about Mother's driving by talking about their forthcoming trip to San Francisco, where Mr. Nesbitt was going to bid on some construction supplies. They were staying in the best hotel, whose name she couldn't remember. Mother, fussy about hotels and knowing the San Francisco ones well, refrained from helping her out.

There where the road goes up the hill, start slowing down. Dad does it in second gear, all the way to the station.

I leaned further over the back of the seat so I could see the gauges. The needles were all more or less in the middle so I guessed everything was all right. A cottontail darted across the road. Mother slammed on the brakes, skidded to the right, then corrected in time to keep from heading off into the sagebrush.

Do they have a restroom at the store? Mrs. Nesbitt asked, almost shouting.

I'd use the one at the train station across the street, Mother said.

On the other side of the hill Basalt Junction lay sprawled out before us, such as it was: the wooden station and water tank and a long line of rusty hopper cars on the right. Left, on the other side of the road, the ramshackle tin-roof building that housed Smedley's General Store, twin gas pumps in front, and in back a collection of the many old cars and trucks that had died or been wrecked over several decades within a twenty-mile radius. The space also housed the post office, a bar and pool-room, and restrooms. The walls of the men's restroom were scribbled with graffiti and papered with stained magazine and calendar pinups. Mother imagined these, or so I guessed from Dad's allusions to them, as a threat to my tender sensibilities and urged me to use the bathroom across the street in the station. On trips down here without her, Dad let me go inside though he appeared slightly embarrassed at the buxom pinups and traces of four-letter words carved into the woodwork and defaced in turn by subsequent carvers. Next to the smelly urinal were two condom dispensers bolted to the wall, the first I had ever seen, and when I asked Dad what they were, he replied while bending over to wash his hands, Those, well, those are something for grown-ups . . . The men's restroom of Smedley's General Store haunted me through my early adolescence as a kind of Neolithic cave filled with traces of strange rites and sacrifices I was still far from comprehending. Was that where, I now wondered, Frank's *masturbation papers* were issued?

I reminded Mother that she should get gas. She pulled up in

front of the pumps and switched off the engine. Mrs. Nesbitt swung open her door and climbed out and headed across the dirt road, her long navy-blue skirt whipping around her heavy ankles. Frank followed in a waddling run.

Mr. Smedley finally pushed through the screen door and lurched over to the pump and cranked the numbers back to zero.

Mr. Alton up at the mine, I suppose, he said. He was a stooped old man with gray hair that stood out in tufts as if he had slept badly on it and not combed it back into place.

And how is Mrs. Smedley?

Damned if I know. Stopped talking to me last year. You want me to fill her up, Mrs. Alton?

And could you—? What else should he do, Scotty?

Oil, tires, I suggested. That is what Dad has Mr. Smedley do.

Don't even need to ask, he muttered. You have a Special Delivery parcel, Mrs. Alton. I wanted to send it up on the train yesterday but she wouldn't let me. If she was talking to me she would have told me it was against the rules and that she had to hand it to you in person, post-office rules, and not turn it over to some perfect-stranger railroad conductor she's only known forty years but who she might never see again. That's what she would have said. But as I said, she's not talking to me.

Mother climbed out of the car and made her way around several large potholes filled with greasy water from recent rains and went inside the store. I followed her. In the back of my mind I was trying to figure out how I could get my ruby back from Frank. I always expected to find everything the same inside the cavernous space with its oily plank floors, the clinging smell of kerosene, shelves of dusty canned goods, bottles of soda pop standing upright in the room-temperature water of an open-lid cooler that no longer worked, a smudged glass dairy cabinet with waxed cartons of milk, packages of lunch meat and hot dogs, sliced cheese, and next to it a mostly empty bread rack. Most of the brands were different than those in the grocery store we shopped at in Denver, suggesting that they came from another more exotic commercial universe than the one I was familiar with. Long rows of hardware bins screened off the bar and pool table area. To one side of the entrance, in a gap in the bins, was a rack of two-month-old hunting and fishing and "true adventure" magazines with covers featuring snarling mountain lions and bears and statuesque elk and deer and moose. And also squeezed into the gap there was something new: a circular rack thinly populated with detective paperbacks, with covers of young women only slightly more clad than the pinups in the men's room, in poses of seductive distress. I had enough money to buy one of the twenty-five-cent volumes but was too shy to do so in Mother's presence. Perhaps the next trip down with Dad, or later, back at home, in Denver, at the corner drugstore, which might carry them by then.

Mother was pushing a squeaky shopping basket up and down the aisles and bending over and squinting at the can labels in the gloom when Mrs. Nesbitt and Frank came in the door. After noting the telltale bulge in his right pants pocket, I quietly slipped out. Mr. Smedley was poking around under the hood of the LaSalle. Across the road, the station counter was closed and nobody was inside the waiting room; the morning train, which we had probably passed during a stretch where the road and the tracks were separated by a mile or so of rolling hills, would be puffing up the hill toward the lodge about now. I walked through the board-and-batten structure painted a dull orange both inside and out. On the other side, I stepped down to the tracks and sat down on one of the rails opposite a tangled stack of used ties and another pile of plate-sized squares of rusty steel. Just down the tracks stood a water tower whose redwood slats were bound together by giant iron hoops; water seeped and dripped from a dozen places, staining the wood with smears of rust and streaks of algae. Further beyond there was an elevated coal hopper with a chute that could be lowered over the coal tender behind the engine. Railroad machinery had always fascinated me, feeding a never-confessed (and never to be realized, I am sure) ambition to someday own a whole railroad. I was not yet entirely aware of the paradox of having quite the opposite feeling toward the mine, whose basic processes seemed loud and explosive in threatening ways. Now it intrigued me that I could sit here amid all this grand paraphernalia for hours at a time, if I wanted to, and that in that time virtually nothing might happen. The station master might finally wander in, raise the counter hatch, send a telegram, doze off; or a conductor might show up to board the late-afternoon train, perhaps even with a passenger or two. All would wait and wait here for the eventual arrival of the next train, with its flamboyant eruptions of steam and smoke and its symphony of rhythmic noises, a presence that might last for no more than half an hour. Once recharged with water and coal, it would roll away and disappear around a bend, restoring the scene to sleepy quiet again for the rest of the evening and through the night. A major junction had once been planned for here, I later learned, and the place had been named accordingly, but changing fortunes in the railroad business had deprived the name, Basalt Junction, of its reason for being.

While I sat there a lone sparrow pecked at something at the end of the asphalt platform; other than that, nothing happened. I imagined Frank standing in the store, his right hand fingering my ruby through the cloth of his pants. I got up, brushed myself off, walked back through the station. Mr. Smedley was putting air in the tires. Inside, Mother was waiting at the counter to pay for her groceries and the gas and pick up her parcel. In the basket was a Baby Ruth. She would be buying it to console me for having to spend time with Frank and to spare me from spending any of my allowance. I looked away, pretending I hadn't seen it.

Frank was thumbing through old comic books on a rack near the windows. I never even looked at them anymore. Mrs. Nesbitt was walking slowly up and down the narrow aisles, her nose in the air.

This store certainly does not carry much merchandise, she said in a loud voice to no one in particular.

I stepped back outside just as Mr. Smedley was coming in. I climbed into the backseat of the LaSalle. A minute later Frank opened the other door and got in.

I'm going to get even, I said in a low voice, staring at him, then turning away.

For what?

Stealing my ruby.

I didn't steal it, I found it.

Yeah, where? In the river?

No, on the floor under my bed.

And so how did it get there?

I guess it fell.

Or got pushed.

No, I rolled over in my bed and banged against the wall and then it dropped down from your bunk and slid down—

The car jostled. Mr. Smedley was loading boxes and sacks into the trunk. The women opened the front doors and climbed in. Mother waited for Mr. Smedley to slam the trunk door closed before starting the engine. Frank slouched down in the seat, both hands in his pockets. Oddly I felt he might be telling something like the truth. I had never shown him or spoken about the ruby. The concealing knot did sometimes just fall out, often in the middle of the night, perhaps in response to my rolling over and hitting the wooden wall. But the ruby was still mine, and he still had it, and if he hadn't actually stolen it he probably would have tried to had he known of its existence.

Just give it back, I hissed over the whine of the gears.

No.

Mrs. Nesbitt twisted around. What did you say, Scotty?

Nothing, Mrs. Nesbitt.

She held her eyes on me a moment and turned halfway around and asked Mother, So this is the nearest—you call this a *town*?

A few more people live up at Bessy's Lake, at least in the summer, but the road up there is so bad, Mother said. I hear they're going to reopen the hotel.

So this is it.

Mother didn't respond, nor did she add that Mr. Smedley always drew Dad aside to whisper dirty jokes to him, or often the same joke over and over again, in response to which Dad forced out embarrassed smiles and which, as far as I knew, he never repeated or spoke of other than to observe that this was

The fifth time he's told that one. I leaned forward and resumed my role as lookout for road hazards. Mother was driving too fast, forgetting the hills ahead. I coached her to slow down, back into second gear. All the while I was imagining how to get my ruby back in some clever way that wouldn't involve either Mother or Mrs. Nesbitt. Frank surely knew he was far more vulnerable to punishment than I was. As far as I knew I had the reputation of being a "good" kid who rarely got into trouble. My only memory of punishment was a spanking by Dad when I was very young, a searing experience that served to keep me out of trouble for most of my early childhood. I sensed that Mrs. Nesbitt was hypersensitive to any seeming misbehavior by Frank; she was aware of his every movement and word.

We passed the fork that headed to the highway, ten miles of difficult dirt road east, and a boarded-up gas station beyond which stood the blackened wooden sheds and squat conical smokestack of a sawmill that had ceased operations two years ago. A moment later we rumbled over two sets of narrow-gauge track mostly buried in the dirt and overgrown by grass between the road and the sawmill.

We crossed the hills and set off across the rolling plain of scrub oak and sagebrush and the occasional solitary ponderosa pine left over from the long-ago logging of the area. Halfway across the plain we passed a landmark I had missed on the way to Basalt Junction, a rusty hulk of a grand old touring car, all four doors open, its top bows still in place but the canvas rotted away, chrome radiator shell still bright in the sun. Its nose was turned away from the road so I could only guess that it was probably a Packard, maybe a Cadillac, from the late 1920s. As we approached the mouth of the canyon, Mother asked me to watch out for a track through the grass to the left. It led to a clear sandy patch next to the river where the water flowed slowly and smoothly. We often stopped there and picnicked and sometimes swam. At my words, she slowed and turned onto the dirt track that wound through the grass and up over the railroad tracks and down to a clearing beside the water. It was hot but a breeze was wafting out of the mouth of the canyon. We left the doors open to cool down the car.

Did you boys bring your bathing suits? Mother asked.

No, I replied sullenly, taking my sack lunch and moving off some distance to sit down on a grassy bank above the water. Opposite, along the far bank, the river hissed flat and shallow over a bed of small stones. A school of trout fry wiggled and darted in the water just below my feet. Frank walked upstream a ways and sat down and opened his lunch sack. The women leaned against the front fenders and stared out at the scene. The grass around the gravelly clearing had been grazed short and was littered with cow pies, some fresh. I ate my sandwich and cookies quickly and walked back to the car.

Let's go, I said, interrupting Mother. I had a plan to get the ruby back. It depended on my having a moment alone in my room without Frank.

In a minute, she said. She turned back to Mrs. Nesbitt, who held her sandwich up as if to examine it before each bite. When Scotty Senior was young, Mother resumed, there was so much more going on around here. Basalt Junction was almost a proper town. I think he told me it even had a little movie house.

You don't say.

And Bessy's Lake Hotel was supposed to be one of the best

in this part of the Rockies. They ran four trains a day on holidays up through the canyon. Quite the little hub.

Yes, very beautiful at first, but after a while it becomes, well, not so beautiful and a little tiring, I find. Yes, I find all this scenery tires me. Do you find that?

Let's go, I urged.

Frank joined us. I'm still hungry, he said.

Mrs. Nesbitt gave Frank one of her cookies and we climbed back into the car and drove back to the road and headed up the canyon. Halfway back to the lodge at a place where the tracks and the dirt road ran side by side we came across the train stopped on the tracks. A half dozen passengers were standing around and watching the crew squatting under a hopper car and working at something. Mother stopped the car. At the head of the train, the engine chuffed lightly as if it was chewing its cud. Mr. Sanchez, the conductor, walked over and tipped his cap.

Jammed brake shoe, Mrs. Alton. With luck we'll get moving again in a while here, he laughed. This thing should have been turned into scrap for the war effort, if you want my opinion. Mr. Alton coming back tomorrow, I believe?

Mother introduced Mrs. Nesbitt and asked whether there was anything she could do. Mr. Sanchez shook his head, patted the LaSalle on the roof, and strolled back to the disabled hopper car. The immobilized passengers watched us as we pulled away.

Half an hour later we were back at the lodge. I knew Frank and I would be asked to carry the grocery sacks into the kitchen from the garage where Mother parked the car, but if I worked fast enough I could slip away before Frank set down the last one on the kitchen table. I was alert with anticipation while he was groggy from the drive. Instead of joining him to bring in the last sacks I bounded upstairs. I had originally thought to grab his Boy Scout uniform and hide it somewhere in one of the spare rooms but then feared that this might cause an uproar in the house; and I would obviously be the culprit. When I saw his *Boy Scout Handbook* lying facedown on the lower bunk I realized that it would make a much better prize. A quick look confirmed that my hiding-place knot was lying on my bunk near the wall. I snapped up the *Handbook* and tucked it under my shirt, ran down the stairs and across the living room and out the veranda and around behind the house back to the garage. Frank had just stepped inside the back door. The trunk lid was still open but all of the groceries had been carried away. I slipped into the garage, opened the back door of the LaSalle, placed the *Handbook* down on the floor where Frank had been sitting, quietly closed the door, and then walked around to the back of the car and slammed down the trunk lid and walked up the steps into the kitchen.

Was that everything, Scotty?

Yeah. I'm going swimming.

Frank was sitting at the dining room table with his head down, red face cradled in his arms.

Mother looked at him. It's probably the altitude, you know.

You let him go by himself? I heard Mrs. Nesbitt ask.

I ran upstairs, grabbed my swimming trunks, changed in the bathroom, ran back down the stairs and headed for the river. As I loped through the mottled shade of the cottonwoods it felt as if I was already in the water washing away the sweaty grittiness of the uncomfortable morning and would soon completely forget the Nesbitts, at least for a while. I splashed into the faintly muddy water, warmer than when clear, and flopped down and let the current wash over my body. The first thunderheads were clearing the ridge to the east but were still far from obscuring the midafternoon sun. I let myself drift downstream in the shallow water toward the first of the rapids, near my sitting boulder. In the willows overhanging the far bank, something moved. I sat up. A large gray-brown muskrat slipped into the water and disappeared. I lay back for a while until I began to get cold and then slithered up on the warm boulder and stretched out on my stomach in the sun.

Despite her effusions on arriving, it was becoming clear to me that Mrs. Nesbitt was finding the place not to her liking. I had probably been noticing something in guests' behavior for a long time but was now becoming conscious of it: how most soon became uneasy with the overwhelming presence of this rocky, steep landscape, which for me was by contrast a reliable presence, one that I could know and trust and mostly not be afraid of. I knew when and where it could be tricky and dangerous—during thunderstorms, mainly. I had no fear of its thorns, its black widows, even of its rattlers, which I had only encountered twice and from a safe distance, nor its mountain lions and bears, which I had only seen signs of with the help of a biologist friend of the family, who had pointed out their scat on evening walks. The place's creatures, mostly hidden as they were, hovered as a constant presence. I knew where the largest trout hid in the flow, though I rarely saw more than a blurred shape darting through the water; I had a sense of the bird life, some species rarely glimpsed, moving up and down the river course; I was in tune to the ground squirrels, golden-mantled squirrels, kangaroo mice, gray water snakes, the small lizards inhabiting the open sandy spaces around the lodge, the most domestic of all the creatures along with the toads that often positioned themselves outside the back door at night to snap up moths and insects drawn toward the kitchen lights. Visiting geologists like Mr. Slatter made the rocks come alive in new ways, though as a connoisseur from a young age of stones and their shapes and textures and colors, I found that this technical knowledge added little to my own very private categories and hierarchies of what was interesting and beautiful—nor was I suitably impressed by his earnest assertions that all rocks were incredibly old, which, arrogantly, I thought I already knew. I was still a few long human years from understanding the radically expanding concepts of geological time.

I was roused from these musings by a shout from the shore. I lifted my head. It was Mrs. Nesbitt in her high heels and ankle-length navy-blue skirt standing in the sand.

Frank has lost his *Boy Scout Handbook*, she called out. Have you seen it somewhere?

No, Mrs. Nesbitt, I haven't. I was surprised at how easily the lie tripped off my tongue.

He says he left it on his bed. He has to do some studying for the merit badge.

I don't know, Mrs. Nesbitt

She stared across at me for a long moment, her nose in the air as if trying to sniff out the truth, and then turned away and lifted her skirt and walked with wide lurching steps back toward firmer ground. Good, I thought, good. Now we're even.

A foot-long stick had become wedged between the boulder and a smaller rock. I lay back down on my stomach and stretched over the edge and plucked it free and then began waving its point into the weave of the flow, following the effervescent shapes and disturbances it kicked up and watching how it recast wavelets and ridges of water almost too quickly for the eye to follow. I had always found the surfaces of moving water engrossing, particularly close up, and now remembering an explanation I had not understood at the time given by Mr. Wilcox, who came into class once a week to talk about science, I could imagine the flow of water as a demonstration of the pull of gravity—as if the crest of each wavelet or the depth of each trough were attached to a string tugging it downward deep into the core of the earth. The rocks and boulders perched above on the canyon walls also came to be attached to invisible strings straining to pull them down; when summer downpours loosened the soil beneath, then they would submit to the tug of gravity and come tumbling down. That's why we bury dead people in the ground, he had explained during one class. We give them back to gravity. For a day or two following his explanation I willed myself to crumple up and fall again and again on the new living room carpet of the Denver house—until Mother finally said, Are you all right? Maybe I should take you to the doctor. I explained I was just testing the pull of gravity.

Scotty?

I lifted my head, turned. Now Mother was standing on the beach. Are you sure you didn't take Frank's Boy Scout book?

Yes! I shouted back in an angry voice, satisfied with my feigned vehemence. She turned and walked back toward the lodge, the strings of gravity pulling her more strongly on her right side. I imagined the scene inside: Frank throwing a tantrum, red-faced, shouting, whimpering that he needed to finish the merit badge before school and how the scoutmaster would reprimand him for losing the *Handbook* or how Mr. Nesbitt would slip his belt from his waist and whack him, strings of gravity helping snap the leather strap down on the plump behind.

Thunderheads were gathering higher over the ridge but the western sun still angled into the depths of the canyon. I rolled off the rock for a last dip before the sky clouded over, anchoring myself against the flow. Through the cottonwoods I made out a flash of red swimming trunks. Frank stepped from the shadows and plodded across the sand and stood at the edge of the water, hands on hips, face flushed.

You stole my *Handbook*! he shouted. Where is it?

I didn't either steal it. It was lying on my bed. I found it.

Where is it?

Give me back my ruby and I'll tell you.

I climbed back on to the warm boulder just as clouds obscured the sun. The beach was swept by a gust of wind coming down the canyon. The upper branches of the cottonwoods waved back and forth wildly for a moment. I wondered whether air was subject to gravity, whether there were strings reaching up into the sky and attached to clouds. But of course, each raindrop had a little string attached to it. When it rained, you could almost see them.

Okay, he finally said.

Put my ruby on my bunk bed and then I'll tell you where your *Handbook* is, okay?

No, you give me back my *Handbook* and then I'll give you back the ruby.

No.

Frank looked across at me for a moment through swollen

eyelids. Okay, he said, turning and walking back through the trees.

I waded back to shore and dried myself off and ran barefoot back up to the lodge, up the steps and across the living room and up the stairs. Frank was sitting on the lower bunk, the chunk of deep-red cut glass lying on the top bunk. I snapped it up and told him to go downstairs and I'd call down where the *Handbook* was. I didn't want to risk him pulling a hammerlock on me and wrestling it away. As soon as he left I thrust the ruby into the bottom of the pillowcase that served as my laundry bag, shoved it under the lower bunk, then stuck my head out and shouted, In the backseat of the LaSalle, on the floor where you left it.

I got dressed and ran downstairs with my book and claimed a wicker armchair on the veranda to watch the storm roll in. Mother was in the kitchen. As I walked past, I called out, He found his book.

Where?

In the car.

But having my ruby back was anticlimactic. Somehow it was no longer that important, no longer contained the magical powers I had once tried to wish into it. Perhaps Rosalind's apathy toward it, or even Frank's covetousness, had discharged the aura. It was only a large red piece of cut glass, chipped in two places, and not good for anything. I even forgot about it until a couple of days after the Nesbitts had left, when Mother decided to wash some clothes for the drive back to Denver and she emptied my laundry into the old Maytag wringer washer on the back porch and the ruby came clunking out on to the floor.

What's this doing in the laundry bag? Mother asked absently, handing it back to me in the kitchen.

The men came back the next morning just before noon, the Packard splattered with mud. The Nesbitts left shortly after. Mr. Nesbitt hadn't liked what he had seen at the mine and stopped talking about investing in it, and Mrs. Nesbitt's initial enthusiasm for the lodge and the scenery had been supplanted with phrases like *so isolated, so far away from everything.* Frank had become fearful that I might steal one of the gold-plated pins on his Boy Scout uniform before he left but this time not give it back, not knowing that I dreaded even touching the material. After the Nesbitts left, Mother and Dad spent the next several days closing down the lodge, shutting off the water, fastening the shutters, and loading boxes of food and clothing into the LaSalle. I read, paddled in the river, and fastened strings of gravity to everything I saw. As the LaSalle labored up the hill in low gear toward the tracks for the last time that summer, I watched the strings grow longer and longer—and finally snap.

Four

DURING WINTER DRY spells Mrs. Smedley drove an old
Chevy pickup up the canyon to check on the lodge, parking at
the top of the hill to avoid getting stuck on the often-icy driveway. She left packets of meat scraps upstairs for the feral cat
that lived in the attic. A hatch in the upstairs hallway ceiling
was propped open and a rickety stepladder positioned under it
so the cat could come down and patrol the rooms for mice and
squirrels. Mrs. Smedley also set and emptied mouse traps in the
oven and refrigerator, whose doors she left ajar but not wide
enough for the cat to climb inside. On the way back up to the
lodge for the summer we stopped at the store in mid-June to
pick up the keys and ask how the winter had gone and whether
everything was okay at the lodge. We were particularly con-
cerned because we had skipped last summer when Mother was
recuperating from an operation; although the mine had remained partially shut down, Dad had made three trips up to it

all the way from Denver by train and a couple by car. He hadn't stayed at the lodge, which wouldn't have been worth opening up for a night or two.

Everything fine, Mrs. Smedley said, not being in one of her talkative moods. She was a big woman with gray hair pulled back into a bun, and she was never without a canvas apron with pockets for change cinched tight over her flat breasts and ample stomach.

All she means, Mr. Smedley grunted, was that the bear that broke down the kitchen door and tore up all the upholstery—

Shut your mouth.

Mother and Dad were not certain whether Mr. Smedley had been joking or not. The rest of the drive was punctuated by musings about whether there had in fact been a bear or not and if so how much damage it had done and whether it had got to the mattresses, and where we were going to sleep if it had. By the time we arrived I was imagining the lodge filled with tufts of white kapok and gray feathers, lumps of bear scat all over the floors. The last things that got packed away before we left were our bedding and pillows, which went into wooden and metal war-surplus footlockers with servicemen's names still stenciled in white on them, and I wondered whether the bear, or now bears, could pry them open and tear their contents apart as well. The Slatters had told stories of bears in camp-grounds where people had unwisely locked food inside their cars for safekeeping, and how the bears climbed up on the roofs and jumped up and down on the wood and canvas panels of the older cars until they collapsed. I was glad our 1940 LaSalle had a solid steel roof.

From outside, everything looked unchanged, except a

cottonwood had toppled over across the driveway turnaround, some of its larger limbs just missing the veranda roof and wooden railings of the stairs. Shattered branches lay scattered in a wide radius. But this we didn't see until after we had entered the house from the back door and had begun going around outside to unlatch shutters. Mr. Smedley had been joking: no bear had gotten inside. Other than the remains of a mouse in the kitchen and a pile of feathers that had once been a flicker—I wondered why the cat had dragged the bird downstairs—everything seemed normal, that is, dusty and smelling of mold and cat pee. We opened all the doors and windows to the late-morning breezes and sunlight. The rest of the day we spent unpacking the LaSalle and dragging the thin mattresses and bedding outdoors to air in the sun, then getting everything in place before dark.

Our first guests were to have been the Slatters but at the last minute they reversed the order of their visit and would be calling by on their way back from Yellowstone, not on their way up. I had spent the past two years building elaborate fantasies around Rosalind, how we would be so talkative now that we were old friends from her visit the summer before last, our long separation giving us so much to talk about. I had even passed through Pomona on a train trip to Los Angeles at Christmastime last winter, and not just once, but twice. From the train window I had studied the industrial strip along the tracks and hilly residential areas rising up the slopes beyond with the attentiveness of a seasoned expert, though in fact I had no idea of what I was looking at or even looking for, other than she probably lived somewhere in the distant haze. It was an irrelevant detail that the Slatters were probably away from home themselves during Christmas vacation. Certainty lay only in the fact that I had taken the Union Pacific City of Los Angeles through Pomona twice over Christmas on the way to Catalina Island and back to Cheyenne, and it offered the possibility of providing material for future hours of banter and conversation with Rosalind.

I have to sit on this side, I hissed to Mother, pressing my forehead to the tinted glass. We were traveling coach, as what was to have been our sleeping car had been pulled from the train because of a plumbing problem.

But it's not our seat, she objected.

Then I'll move when they come back.

When the train was delayed at the Pomona station on the way into Los Angeles, I was convinced that the Slatters had cancelled their vacation plans and that they had been unable to reach Dad and Mother before we had left Denver for the Cheyenne station, they were desperate to find us, Mrs. Slatter was about to drive into the station parking lot, Rosalind would climb out of their Studebaker and begin scanning the windows for my face. She would break into a smile, a smile I had to imagine as I had never seen her truly smile before, and wave, mouthing my name, Scotty, I see Scotty, she would be saying, beckoning Mrs. Slatter over. After patting down an erection (a term a classmate had recently provided for my private glossary, though I was still not certain it referred to what I was actually experiencing), a regular feature now of riding in a car or train for more than ten minutes, I would get up from my seat and rush down the aisle through the automatic door and in the gloom of the vestibule I would smash the glass of the little hatch behind which dangled the bright-red emergency-brake handle, oddly penis-like, and reach in and pull it. That way Rosalind and I could have enough time together before the train moved off toward its destination. The thought ended when the train lurched forward, halted with a hiss and a bang, then resumed its course, my erection firm and steady beneath the spread-out pages of my book turned upside down on my lap.

My erogenous zones were not yet connected to my consciousness, at least in a direct way, but as I walked through the long trains between Denver and Los Angeles and Chicago on our frequent trips, particularly at night when the lights were dimmed and the Vista Dome car was filled with smokers nursing cocktails and beers as they peered out past their reflections in the glass at points of light slipping by in the darkness, I came to imagine all the other boys and men on the train sitting with their penises rigid, defying gravity and pointing skyward, even the engineer and the fireman as they sat staring straight ahead in the darkened cab of the throbbing diesel-electric locomotive, penises guiding them compass-like through the night. As I walked up and down the aisles in the gloom, cars rollicking and lurching, I sought the confirmation of tent-like shapes in the material of slacks and jeans of the sprawled half-dozing and snoring passengers, but found little. Either everyone was as good at concealing their condition as I was or else I was the only one afflicted with it.

This last explanation seemed most likely. I was too embarrassed to ask anyone, let alone Mrs. Sanders, a new teacher who had presided over the "health education" film that kept breaking just when I had hope of clarification. It was all so diagrammatic and abstract, narrated by a deep-voiced, confident, expert-sounding man, with long hopeful words and upbeat music, that when Mrs. Sanders turned the lights back on and pulled up the blinds, she could have seen from the shifty eyes and glassy stares and the unusual silence of the room—the film was shown to two grades together—that most of us were more confused than ever. *Sex* was not yet a term in common use except when referring to the gender of kittens and puppies, and the definition of *erection* in the family dictionary, as revealed by a furtive thumbing search while Mother was busy in the kitchen fixing dinner, offered an exasperating list of apparent circumlocutions, the most vivid of which was "to raise and set in an upright or perpendicular position: *to erect a telegraph pole.*" Back in front of the hot, overcrowded classroom, after retracting the screen back up into its blue metallic housing with a series of awkward jerks, Mrs. Sanders wrung her hands together and asked, Any questions? There were none. Afterward out on the playground during recess, girls and boys drifted apart, no one said anything to anyone, at least among the boys I knew, though there was some huddling among the girls. There were no whispered conversations, smirks, red faces, guffaws. Remarkable as it came to seem decades later, the stalls of the boys' bathroom were scrawled with nothing more risqué than *Joseph loves Rhonda.* Not long after, at the recollection of the term *fallopian tubes* and the severe line drawings that represented them, I thought of Mother's Electrolux canister vacuum, though it only had one hose, not two. As a six-year-old I used to follow her around as she vacuumed, waiting for her to tell me when to press down on the raised, fin-like foot switch at the rear of the metallic brown canister, to turn the machine on and off. I was too young to see its vaguely clitoral aspect: that came much later, in recollection.

My anticipation of Rosalind's return toward the end of the month cast a warm glow over the mundane business of getting the lodge up and functioning, the water from the spring turned on, bathroom heater working again (Mr. Smedley had promised to replace its tall propane bottle in a couple of days), mummified mouse removed from the oven trap, droppings swept up from the floor, cobwebs finally brushed down from the ceiling rafters with a broom wired to a pole, windows washed, rugs hung out to air, wooden floors mopped over with Lysol to get rid of the animal smells. Dad put me to work with a bow saw cutting up the smaller branches of the dead cottonwood out front into firebox lengths for the kitchen range, work that easily tired me and for which I invented excuses to leave off so I could go back to reading on the veranda. He was not a very physical man himself, and I took some pleasure in noting that he often spent less time sawing branches than I did. Eventually Mr. Smedley, after having delivered the propane, returned with two young men, who quickly bucked up the tree with a long two-man saw and then split the rounds into firebox size with mauls and wedges. I glanced down at them from time to time over the top of my book. They worked smoking and shirtless in the heat of late morning, communicating with each other in monosyllables and generally ignoring Mr. Smedley's repertory of (from what little I could hear) dirty cracks and jokes. With muscular arms and wisps of chest and underarm hair they seemed like another species, different from anything I might ever become. Midafternoon they climbed into Smedley's old Chevy pickup and drove off. Just as they were swinging around in the turnaround in front of the lodge, one of the young men hawked a gobbet of spit in a graceful arc out the open window into a clump of lilac. Later, down at the beach, I tried to imitate the manly gesture but succeeded only in drooling down my bony, hairless chest.

While down at the store one afternoon I summoned up the courage to ask Mrs. Smedley to give me two silver dollars in exchange for eight quarters I had saved up from my allowance. Silver dollars were becoming rare in Denver and unheard of in Chicago but were still common currency in out-of-the-way places like Basalt Junction. I now walked around the lodge with the two heavy coins making reassuring chinking sounds in my pocket. Now and then I would interrupt my reading to pull them out and study the liberty heads, the eagles, the inscriptions, and I would clank them together in my palm for the sounds they made. Noticing me one afternoon, Dad suggested that the silver might have come from our own mine, possibly the 1882 coin, whose tiny *D* indicated it was minted in Denver, but less likely for the 1921 coin, whose *S* below the arrows clutched in the eagle's claws stood for the San Francisco mint.

In the first days of cleaning out the lodge Dad and Mother were unusually contented. Mother forgot in her busyness that she really didn't like being here, and since Dad had not visited the mine in nearly three months its concerns had been pushed aside by the details of getting the lodge clean and comfortable again. I pitched in more than was expected of me, though all the fussing over dust on the windowsills and ripped window shades seemed quite unnecessary, as did washing the perfectly clean cutlery and dishes not once but twice. Mother believed that mice and other creatures had spent the winter licking every available surface.

I can't stand to eat from silverware and plates that have been licked by animals, she once snapped at Dad.

Licked?

Slobbered over.

For her, this was extreme language. The image of large slobbering mice, or rats, though in fact we had never seen rats, became a refrain during the lighter moments of the summer, particularly after Aunt Ruby picked it up and carried it to new heights: Perhaps we could send some of these large slobbering rats to the Chicago zoo. By then Mother was regretful that the words had ever crossed her lips. She looked away whenever the conversation turned to the real and imagined fauna of the lodge, usually set off by the sound of something scampering or scratching in the ceiling. There they go again, those large slobbering rats, someone would invariably observe.

After four or five days of tidying up Mother sank back into her old ways, took long naps, slept badly at night, fixed lunch and dinner at unpredictable hours. Dad took up fly-fishing again after many years of neglect and was surprisingly good at it: we ate trout almost every night for a week. In the evening he caught up with his mining journals, a cardboard box of which he had brought along, and went over accounts from the mine at the dining room table. I read on the veranda, hiked up the hill with Dad to await the morning train, then went down to the beach when the morning warmed up, paddled in the water, explored up and down the canyon, discovered a group of Indian petroglyphs on the side of a huge slab of basalt. It was a hot summer; I lived in my bathing trunks, soon turned brown.

Dad left me alone. Perhaps uncertainties about his own life, a sense of looming disappointment, problems at the mine, a natural shyness, one or all restrained him from bestowing advice on me or trying to guide me in a particular direction, unlike other fathers I knew who laid down fixed paths for their sons to follow. I felt this most piercingly when we were waiting together for the morning train up from Basalt Junction, up on the tracks above the lodge, where I often sat on a rail waiting to feel the vibrations of the approaching train, while Dad leaned against a boulder smoking a Lucky Strike, hunched forward and staring at the ground. I had begun to notice chests: he had a narrow, hollow one, from which a deep cough now and then emerged. He spat directly at the ground, to one side, not like the show-off woodcutter. During these often-long waits I expected him to say something, offer some advice, criticize me, tell me a story, point out some unusual detail of the landscape, express some worry about the mine, the lodge, Mother, Aunt Ruby, Walter. The silences yawned sometimes as long as an hour, particularly when some problem arose with the locomotive or one of the cars, even after we thought we had heard the train enter the canyon a couple of miles below. My silences nestled perfectly into his, though I could not know whether he too was seared with a sense of longing and whether in fact it matched my own in any way. I was far from knowing that older people often yearn for just what the young are longing to escape from.

On the end of a wooden cabinet next to the back door of the lodge there was tacked a train schedule, yellowed and curling with age. With amusing precision it listed a *9:53 Canyon Stop [Flagged]* but in reality the train was considered *on time* if it was an hour or less late; *late* meant several hours or half a day. When at last the morning train rounded a corner a half mile below where we waited, Dad would say, There she comes, foreclosing for the rest of the day all possibility of conversation. Five minutes remained. I hung on his gestures: the jerky shooting up of a cigarette from the crumpled packet, the tapping of the cigarette on his wrist, the inserting of it into the corner of his mouth, the tearing of a cardboard match from a packet, the striking of it, the cupping of the palm over the end of the cigarette, the puff of sweet-smelling smoke, the waving of the spent match, which he flicked onto the tracks. The minutes passed. I waited for a question, a remark, anything, before the black locomotive with its grimy silver snout rounded the last bend and gave a quick acknowledging toot of the whistle. I waited and waited. People in the novels I read talked all the time, they seemed never at any loss for words, even if half the time they weren't the right ones and got them into trouble. When I was around other people, particularly adults, I observed who talked and who was silent, and became alarmed when everyone fell into silence at once. Misery ended when someone picked up the conversation and it resumed. I wanted to cheer, Onward, keep going, don't stop, don't stop talking.

After ten days alone with nothing more than brief daily exchanges with the conductor, Mr. Sanchez, and one trip back to Basalt Junction to pick up a food order, Mrs. Smedley as sullen as ever, it felt as if all the silence in the world was descending on the lodge, yet a noisy silence, as my mind was filled with the chattering of the characters in *Vanity Fair* and Mother's unvoiced laments and whatever was flowing around inside Dad's bald head, perhaps charts of numbers from the accounts and tunneling records from the mine. We lacked Aunt Ruby. She never let anyone stay in their corner alone. She sought everyone out, prodded them, mocked them, amused them, dragged them out of hiding. You don't come to a glorious place like this and then sit around and mope, she'd remark with a sarcastic edge. Or do you?

I still lacked the sense to know that I could break the silence myself anytime I wanted. Often I sat out on the flagstone steps of the veranda after breakfast as the day was beginning to warm and listened to the sounds converging on the lodge from a wide radius, the low gravelly rush of the river from up and down the canyon, birds chirping in the trees, a yellow chat going through its vocal acrobatics out of sight high up in the tallest cottonwood, towhees scratching through the dry leaves at the edge of the driveway, a grasshopper whirring across the glare of sand and gravel at the foot of the stairs, the low buzz of a hummingbird in search of a blossom. Very occasionally the crack and mumble of a loosened rock rolling down the steep slope on the other side of the river would penetrate the muffled wash of the water, and I would look up, upriver from the cottonwoods, and scan the boulders and dead tree trunks for the jackrabbit or even coyote that might have triggered the sound. To my back the lodge creaked, doors opened and closed, footsteps thundered up and down the stairs, dishes clattered in the kitchen, water splashed in the sink, and eventually the dull rumbling whine of the Maytag would rise from the back porch, the slap of water against its paddles. A breeze would occasionally stir the round cottonwood leaves, twirling them back and forth, sounding like a shallow stream before dropping back into silence. But voices, no, nothing. There had been other times like this at the lodge, I remembered, and they had lasted until the spell had been broken by the arrival of houseguests or a dramatic occurrence like an injury or a storm. Once the silences were over, I forgot them—until the next period of silence resurrected all the former ones and they joined together into a continuum that blotted out everything else.

At least now I could read my way through this one. The Slatters were due in three days. I calculated I would finish the Thackeray that afternoon. Like all the editions of the bound series on the sagging shelves of the lodge library, it was a slightly condensed and bowdlerized version. I discovered this a few years later in college while reading an unexpurgated version of *Gulliver's Travels*, in which Gulliver puts out the fire in Lilliput by pissing on it. After Thackeray, I would launch into a volume of the stories of Chekhov. Rosalind inhabited a precise place in my imagination, yet had become a blur in the long absence, a shifting composite of the heroines of Hardy, Butler, Austen, and Thackeray. She took on their characteristics in a completely random and shifting way as my eyes raced across the printed words, her fictitious attributes sloughed off and replaced by new ones in each succeeding volume. I had no doubt I would recognize her the moment she stepped out of the family Studebaker, yet I also had no sense that I might have to make major adjustments to my preconceptions, that I would have to alter the vision of a buxom young woman and a strapping young man gliding toward each other, mouths agape, breathless, toward—exactly what? Far from mind was the thought that I might find myself once again to be the skinny tongue-tied kid who could never count on his fits of boldness to come at the right moment, or that Rosalind might seem small and pinched, sullen from the long hot drive, and in no mood to be nice and polite, like her mother usually managed to be, let alone ardent.

My inklings of the complexity of this impending re-encounter were as vague and shifting as the phantom Rosalind herself.

The day before the Slatters were due I awoke to a sound I first took for the rumbling of a distant thunderstorm or the approach of a train on the tracks above the lodge, neither of which were likely at six in the morning. As I became more awake, I realized the sound was coming from down the hall: Mother and Dad were talking again, probably still lying in bed. I could make out no words but listened to the rise and fall of the muffled voices with a sense of warmth and contentment punctuated by moments of panic when they fell silent again. But they soon resumed and I came to accept their brief silences as an element in the natural rhythm of their conversation. I fell back into a deep sleep.

Rosalind, taller, had grown breasts: they reduced me to silence.

What are you reading? was her greeting to the air surrounding me, while Mr. Slatter described obstacles in the form of boulders and gullies they had encountered on the dirt road from the highway to Basalt Junction, with elaborate gestures and guffaws. Their two-tone Studebaker was coated with dust. Peter, unchanged as a happy squirrel of a boy, came around from the other side of the car and urged his father to tell us about *the landslide*. Mrs. Slatter, with a wide smile of greeting, looked as if she wanted to hug Mother but thought better of it. We were all standing next to the hot Studebaker and the canvas-covered trailer in front of the lodge and the pile of newly bucked-up cottonwood logs.

I wasn't certain how to pronounce *Chekhov*, though it seemed obvious enough; I let too much time pass before answering.

Some stories by somebody, I said.

Rosalind had stuck her head back into the car and probably didn't hear.

Do we have to sleep in tents that will get all wet again? she demanded of her mother, setting off a sharp but brief exchange in hushed tones.

Maybe the children could sleep on the veranda, if they'd like, Mother suggested with her usual uncertainty. That would be all right, wouldn't it, Scotty?

Dad waved his consent. I was excited. This would mean Rosalind would be more accessible than she had been out in the pup tent. The veranda was my territory, I could come and plop down on the wicker swing or in one of the armchairs whenever I felt like it. Though this would require me to deal with my tendency to step aside whenever she seemed to be approaching or when she turned her plastic-rimmed glasses in my direction, even when I was not an object of her attention. Her new breasts added a troubling authority to her vagueness. They were confident little orbs, not yet large. They seemed to guide her through space in ways her eyes did not. In school where there was ample opportunity to contemplate my teachers' breasts for hours at a time, I had come to regard them as navigational devices or bodily radar that women moved into place to back up a look or a command, or that somehow picked up signals undetectable to the ear, enabling women to home in on a source of irritation or disruption. They were huge covered eyes that gave women, particularly large-breasted women, special powers. Mrs. Vinsent, my fourth grade teacher, a stocky woman with huge breasts clothed in a navy-blue suit jacket she wore every day, would move closely in on a misbehaving student until her breasts were inches away, her whole body trembling at the effort to restrain them from crushing the offender's head between them, or so I imagined. Rosalind still had only inklings of this power, but it was luring Peter into subtle confrontations in the form of frequent pokings with his fingers or sticks found out in the yard, though never directly at the soft new shapes.

Much of this I worked out in watching the Slatters unpack their car and trailer and set up the tent for the adults. Rosalind and Peter installed themselves at opposite ends of the veranda. Rosalind blockaded herself in the northern corner by standing her suitcase on end and stacking the rolled-up pup tent on top of it as a low wall to screen her sleeping bag from view, which she extended with a cardboard box of books and on top of which she perched a pink leather vanity case Peter had already tried to run away with.

Why did you have to go and lose the key? she called out sharply to Mrs. Slatter, who was on her way through the veranda to the kitchen with a metal ice chest.

To what? her mother called back. But Rosalind's head had already sunk back below her wall. In the wicker chair I was pretending to be absorbed by Chekhov, noisily turning pages back and forth without reading. In his corner, just over the hatch of the basement crawl space, Peter set up a catapult in the form of a flat board laid across a cylindrical stone, with which he intended to launch small piñon cones the length of the veranda toward Rosalind's fortress. His first noisy shots bounced off the wooden ceiling above his head and the less vigorously launched ones fell well short. When he ran out of cones, he threw himself down on his sleeping bag and fell abruptly asleep.

What are you reading? I called out in Rosalind's direction.

What?

What are you reading?

I'm reading all of Dickens.

This was not promising. I had tried to read Dickens but was put off by his use of dialect. The long shelf of his novels in the book room reproached me. But I persisted: Why?

Because I love his books, silly, came from behind the barricade.

But why?

Her face popped up above the suitcase and pup-tent roll and she flicked her dark eyes briefly in my direction. Can't you see I'm reading? she said before sinking back out of sight.

Mr. Slatter tramped up the stairs with a small canvas bag of rolled-up sheets of paper dangling from one hand and paused inside the screen door. He was dressed in wooly green swimming trunks with a white belt.

Anyone want to go for a swim in the river?

No, Rosalind announced from her retreat.

What about you, young fellow?

Dad and Mrs. Slatter had also changed and were in the kitchen finishing up some iced tea made with the last of the ice from the Slatters' cooler. Our refrigerator rarely ran cold enough to make more than slush. Mrs. Slatter's calves were of a startling fullness. Mother was still dressed. Though her operation had taken place almost a year ago, I heard her explain to Mrs. Slatter, she felt it was too soon to go in the water. I ran upstairs and put on my trunks made of a rubbery blue satin material, fearful that the outline of my genitals would show as dramatically as the men's, even in their now timidly shrunken state. On the path through the cottonwoods I caught up with the adults walking slowly single file. Mr. Slatter was telling a story about when they were all young together at the beach drinking bootleg beer around a fire, just after Dad began dating Mother. I found it hard to imagine Mother and Dad ever sitting around a fire on the sand; they almost never went to the river anymore, even on the hottest days. Aunt Ruby was the only one who ever took me to the Lake Michigan beaches in Chicago, and once to a beach in Santa Monica.

They laid out blankets on the edge of a sunny patch of sand. Dad looked almost sunken and frail next to Mr. Slatter's athletic form, and his wisp of black chest hair was nothing compared to the broad reddish mat that covered Mr. Slatter's chest. Mother sat herself down and wrapped her skirt around her legs and a towel around her shoulders, as if it were chilly, while Mrs. Slatter lay down on her stomach on a towel, her calves and strong thighs positioned conveniently for extended viewing out in the bright sun. Mr. Slatter unrolled a large pencil sketch of a geological study of the area of the mine that had flooded two years ago, holding down its corners with small stones. Peter, barefoot and clad in red swimming trunks, shuffled out of the cottonwood shadows and flung himself down on the sand next to his mother and whined something at her.

I waded out to my favorite boulder. It was worn skin-smooth in places by the action of water and smaller rocks bouncing and rubbing against it during floods, its smoothness here and there pitted with bubble shapes created during its volcanic origins. The washing murmur of the river masked the adults' words. Mrs. Slatter was briefly tormented by a horsefly attracted to her legs; after a decisive slap, she reclined back into stillness, chin propped up on elbows as she chatted to Mother. Mr. Slatter unrolled and pinned down a succession of drawings, rolled them back up and replaced them in their canvas bag. Dad sat, arms embracing knees, and stared down at the sheets of paper.

I wished I had brought my book. I liked the unpronounceable Russian names that seemed like terms of a secret code, feeling my way through them as through a thicket of willows or a tangle of dead branches, and wished for the day when I might finally experience the dilemmas and pains that afflicted Chekhov's characters—without yet understanding what most of them were really about. (Later in college, these early readings turned out to actually be of some help, as they gave me a sense of familiarity.) To become an adult seemed to require a huge leap across an as yet indefinably long expanse, a river or even a lake—or definable only in terms of the years of high school and then college that lay ahead, during which the mysterious process might take place. I listened to adults talking about their childhood or youth with a kind of disbelief, suspecting they were being ironic or cryptic or in fact were referring to something that had never actually happened to them. There were photographs, of course, of parents and grandparents dressed in antique fashions, leaning against or sitting inside old-fashioned cars, but what was lacking and what therefore made these images unbelievable was the embracing flow of the then-present moment. Deducing the past from old photos and the shorthand of memory as it appeared in casual conversation among adults seemed like trying to imagine a huge cottonwood from a handful of dry leaves.

At the time I knew these thoughts only as a vague pang occasioned by the presence of adults lying on blankets in their little collective island on the edge of the shallow water, unaware until much later how serious a moment this was for them all. I had intimations, certainly, that this might be my last summer at the lodge, but without any sense of alarm: the change, the ending of summers here, would eventually enfold itself into the larger business of growing up, like the setting aside of toys, certain kinds of clothing, and replacing certain habits—that still-troublesome word—with others. I could imagine that when we drove away from the lodge up the steep drive for the last time in about six weeks I would probably feel no sense of departure or loss of the sort I would learn to dramatize ten or fifteen years later, at least internally; and I wondered whether much later I would even remember the moment I imagined sitting in the backseat of the bouncing LaSalle, probably irritated that I would be unable, for the next minute or so, to read . . .

The river flowed, the sun grew hot, I slipped off the rock into the water, and masked from the others by the boulder, pulled down my trunks and peed, splashed around for a minute, climbed back on the rock. Mother had lain down on the sand, knees up, wrapped in her long skirt. Mr. Slatter was standing and helping his wife to her feet, and together they tiptoed into the water. I watched them through the crook of my elbow as they waded to a deep part of the flow and flopped in and ducked their heads underwater. After a rumbling laugh from him and two quick smiling shrieks from her, they floated off in separate ways and then sat submerged except for their heads, lodged against separate boulders. After a while they stood up in the knee-high water and Peter splashed out through the shallows and flopped down in it briefly. Then they all waded back to shore and rejoined Dad and Mother. Mrs. Slatter's wet calves glistened in the sun.

Eventually a gust of wind rolled down the canyon and black clouds began edging over the high ridge to the east. The others gathered up their blankets and towels and brushed themselves off and sauntered back toward the lodge. Mother and Mrs. Slatter peered in my direction a second, waved, turned away, Peter dancing around his mother's heels. Rosalind would still be reading on the veranda, probably wouldn't notice the others tramping through. How could I attract her attention? I wished Aunt Ruby were here: if she wouldn't exactly tell me, she'd show me through her own actions and words.

Young woman, if only you'd look up from your book now and then you might discover something of interest. Or someone. We're not bumps on a log, you know.

What? Rosalind would respond.

What did you reply to *what* with?

I regained the shore moments before the clouds slid in front of the sun. There was too much lightness to the air for it to rain other than perhaps a brief shower, not like it would when the clouds closed in simultaneously from the west and the air grew heavy with humidity. I walked back up to the lodge but went in through the back door so as not to display my skinny form to Rosalind—I was taller, which made me feel more vulnerable— and went up to my room to change. The space seemed barren and empty compared to those rich moments two summers ago when I had contemplated from below the bulge in the mattress Rosalind made above, after her pup tent flooded. Nothing would dislodge her from her veranda fortress; she would never sleep in my bed again. The bulge had been unexpected, miraculous. I had spent hours observing it from the lower bunk, attentive to its every shift and jiggle, letting it enter and then fill my memory, to the point that for days afterward, or so I remembered in the early-afternoon gloom of my room, the image hung before my eyes blotting out everything else. But because I had not yet fully discovered the power of touch, I had not reached up and palpitated the rough mattress ticking, lightly enough that she would not have felt the tips of my fingers: the missed opportunity now shot through me, a searing slash, and then gradually transformed itself into a heaviness, a weight that threatened to slow down all my movements. Would her visit this summer end the same way, in yet another missed opportunity? But not of some kind of bodily contact, which I found too frightening to contemplate; rather a verbal exchange, an engaging riposte to her *what?* that would cause her to sit up and focus her eyes and actually look in my direction, *What did you just say?*, beginning a conversation that would never end, a conversation that would drive away the pauses and awkwardness and moments of doubt that seemed to afflict all the conversations among adults that I had overheard. I would tell her my secrets, or some of them anyway, and show her my favorite places, my meadow, my boulders, the petroglyphs, even the black widow above the crawl space just inside the hatch door. We would learn to read not in antagonism but in tandem with each other, the sound of the one turning a page would become a secret little signal to the other, not a defiant flick.

But how? To earn this, to achieve this, I would have to become suave and confident and cool-headed, though not quite like those aristocratic German officers cynical toward their cause who Mickey and I used to impersonate, complete with heel clickings and rigid salutes and movie accents. I lacked models. The clothes I had just put back on, a plaid short-sleeved shirt, brown pants with a tear near the cuff, seemed too boyish, something Peter would wear. Everything else in my trunk, clothes that Mother still bought me, were variations of these, some more or less worn than others. A checked sports coat hanging in my closet in Denver, worn to infrequent visits to church, was now far too small for me, and I had not yet become comfortable in a newer one of dark-brown wool, still slightly too large. I decided to leave my shoes and socks off and walk barefoot downstairs, with the still somewhat damp beach towel over my shoulders, for what effect I wasn't certain.

Rosalind was still behind her fortress but sitting up. As I crashed down into one of the wicker chairs, she glanced up.

What are you wearing that towel for? she asked.

What? I said, at a loss for words.

She immediately lost interest, resumed reading. Out of the blue a thought shot through my mind.

I've seen a television, I said.

She looked up again, wrinkled her nose. What do you mean? she asked.

I explained in a telegraphic manner that probably made no sense that when we were in Santa Monica last winter on the way to Catalina, a ham radio friend of Dad's had taken us out to his garage workbench to show us a rack of radio tubes and wires and transformers, in the midst of which sat a long gray funnel-like television tube, on whose tiny three-inch screen there appeared a bluish, snowy test pattern for KTLA, Channel 5. This was several years before sets were widely available commercially.

We had crowded around the thing, the only source of heat in the cold garage. Dad had inspected the ungainly assemblage.

Think it's ever going to be good for anything? Dad had asked.

Who cares? his friend had shrugged. Gives me something to do.

Little of this could I describe to Rosalind's glazed-over stare. It sends pictures, I finally managed, not just words.

Why?

I had no answer for that. The machine was a curiosity. If you had no interest in such things, then that was the end of it. Being a boy, I knew I was supposed to be interested in how things worked and had occasionally pulled the tall console radio out from the wall and studied its innards of humming and heat-blackened radio tubes glowing orange, a miniature city of tall buildings—as they became one night when I turned out all the living room lights. I had worked out the source of light for the glowing round dial, a tiny bulb, and how twisting the dial on the front of the console rotated the interlocking blades of the condenser by means of a loop of waxed string, which had something to do with tuning the signal from the various stations. My investigations went no further than this. Every time we saw Dad's ham radio friend, once every couple of years, he tried to give me lessons on volts, watts, ohms, alternating and direct current, condensers, resistors, rheostats, transformers. At the time I could feel the terms retreating to a part of my brain I would never visit. He was a barrel-chested man with wavy blond-gray hair, who drew too close to me while trying to instruct. He would talk while leaning against his workbench, the fingers of his left hand spread wide on the top of a neat stack of girly magazines, which he would pat for emphasis. He and Dad had been in engineering school together. A rarely driven Chrysler Airflow redolent of motor oil and grease sat in the gloom beyond the reach of the workbench lights.

Outmaneuvered in my conversational gambit with Rosalind, I picked up my book and studied the page without seeing the letters. Eventually they came into focus and I began to read.

The next day the men caught the train up to the mine. Later in the morning Mrs. Slatter announced that we were all going for a hike. She was tired of us all just sitting around and reading. It was time we got out into the great outdoors. Mother excused herself from this duty, claiming she didn't feel well. Rosalind and I at least exchanged glances of hostility at the idea, particularly since Peter had started jumping up and down with enthusiasm.

We'll be back in time for lunch, she informed Mother.

I disliked hikes for their implied regimentation and need for a destination, the plodding up and down dusty rocky trails. I much preferred my solitary rambles in the canyon, with long pauses to inspect a boulder, patches of lichen, the grasses along the edge of the water, the small creatures swimming in and floating on the shallow water. Very occasionally I took a friend, though most were too rowdy, heaving rocks into the water or whacking at things with sticks, chasing after anything that moved. But I hadn't even done this for some time, and Mrs. Slatter's command to go hiking was almost welcomed. I wouldn't be able to read, but neither would Rosalind.

No, you can't go barefoot, Peter. Put on your tennis shoes, Mrs. Slatter called out. We were all waiting for Peter down at the trailer. She was wearing a khaki skirt and a white blouse and dirty white tennis shoes and carrying a paper sack.

Where are they?

I don't know. But go find them.

Where are we hiking?

Nowhere, unless you find your shoes.

Mrs. Slatter turned to me. What do you call that place with the rapids? she asked.

The Sluice Box.

I was relieved. It was only about a twenty-minute walk. I had feared she might want to lead us up one of the steep trails out of the canyon to the Indian ruins, little mounds strewn with pottery shards where Dad had once found two arrowheads.

Peter came out of the veranda with his tennis shoes and sat down on the steps and put them on. Rosalind had placed her book on the front fender of the Studebaker and was catching a last read.

Do I have to go? she whined to her mother. Can I take my book?

Yes you do, and no you can't , young lady.

We set off. Peter skipped and ran ahead waving a stick he'd brought up from the river. Rosalind kept close behind her mother, pushing ahead to her side during wide stretches, whining complaints I couldn't hear. I brought up the rear. The path downriver ambled through an apron of sand and black basalt boulders around which the river flowed to the west and then into a copse of cottonwoods where the water swung back against the east slope of the canyon. The path disappeared in the fine gray sand under the trees and reemerged as a narrow up-and-down dirt track winding through jagged boulders above the rushing water, where the river narrowed as it pressed up against the wall of rock. After a hundred feet or so the path opened out into a widening flat of grass and willows and sand, at the beginning of which lay the rusty remains of an upside-down car from the 1920s, most of the wooden spokes of its wheels rotted away and only a few strips of rubber left of its tires. It was buried in the sand up to its fenders, so you couldn't tell whether it was a touring car or a sedan. Dad said it was probably a Model T Ford that had once belonged to the railroad; it had gone off the road above during an autumn storm sometime after Dad and Ruby and their parents had gone back to Denver for the year. He remembered something about the driver having hit a rock so hard he was thrown out of the car, which proceeded on its own across the tracks and over the edge of the cliff. Summer floods later half-buried it in the sand.

We paused and looked at the rusty hulk. Peter jumped up and down on an upside-down running board. I stared at the thing with new interest. I had seen it on a dozen walks down here over the years but had never paid much attention to it. Now the details of its twisted axles and flattened springs and the joints of the remains of its steering gear seemed oddly fascinating. Rust had eaten holes in the sheet metal and had carved and blistered parts of the frame members to blurred and reduced versions of what they had originally been. There were no traces of paint left. Perhaps it was then that I had some kind of realization, though it could well have been on another walk, earlier, given the possibility that the events of a month from now could have retrospectively colored these memories. I was becoming aware of things in an inchoate manner, and I still felt myself a child in some respects and a fledgling adult, prematurely wise, in others. But it was probably here that I first had thoughts about time as something outside of myself: this car had once belonged to someone, it had been at the center of a life, of movement, it had been brand-new once. Soon it would disappear completely, perhaps under sand and mud deposited by the next flash flood. This was not an occasion for emotion in any form, except a sense of something expanding, stretching.

I caught up with the others. Rosalind had lagged behind her mother in a sandy patch that was slow going. Along here the river had deposited broad swaths of sand and gravel and rocks, which gave way to a long stand of tall cottonwoods. To the left, on the east slope of the canyon, a trickle of water dribbled down a fissure in the black cliff, from a spring halfway between the tops of the trees and the railway line and dirt road above. For years the Forest Service had talked of setting up a public campground here but so far nothing had happened. I drew abreast of Rosalind.

We may lose everything, I said, breathless.

What?

I was uncertain how to proceed. There had been talk again at the dinner table last night, when the adults were having coffee, of the mine *declaring bankruptcy*. I had overheard snatches of the conversation from the veranda where I was reading off and on, my attention alternating between Rosalind sitting upright in her fortress with her back to me in order to catch the light from the single overhead bulb, and the adults in the dining room. The subject was not new: since the flooding problems with the mine two summers before there had been frequent family discussions within my hearing about whether and how and when to *dispose* of the mine. But my familiarity with the term *bankruptcy* came mainly from my reading; I hadn't bothered to look it up since it seemed to be a fancy way of saying *losing everything.*

We may lose everything, I repeated. There was something exciting in the proposition, since I couldn't imagine how we could *lose* all of the many things we owned. How could they be lost, disappear? *Everything* presented similar problems. I knew no one who had *nothing.* There was something unique, even distinguished in the phrase. Like all those people who had disappeared from a ship off the coast of Borneo or somewhere, leaving tables in the dining room all set, wine glasses and coffee cups half-full, suitcases unpacked, hands of cards placed face-down midgame.

Everything, I insisted.

What do you mean? she said.

That's what they were saying last night.

Who?

Dad, to your dad.

I could see the 129 passengers and crew members sitting around in the jungle on tree trunks and rocks, waiting. *Bankrupt.* Would they still have clothes on? Maybe whatever happened to Amelia Earhart had happened to them.

But what did he say?

I was too uncertain of the phraseology to trot out what I thought I had heard. Rosalind had her eyes on me, nose tipped up, staring at me through her black plastic-rimmed glasses, vaguely catlike.

Mrs. Slatter had paused ahead and was turned around waiting for us. Peter was playing peekaboo behind tree trunks.

As we approached, I said in a low voice, It's supposed to be a surprise.

What?

But *surprise* was probably the wrong word. It came to me then that adults commonly used the phrase *lost everything* to refer to the Crash and the Depression, though that in fact clarified nothing for me. It had happened before I was born. My parents talked about people who had *lost everything* but it wasn't anyone who came to the house or who we went to visit on weekends; presumably such people were sitting around on a jungle island waiting to get their things back.

After the grove of cottonwoods, the trail switchbacked down a steep slope, where it ended on a wide ledge above the churning Sluice Box fifty feet below. Mrs. Slatter cautioned us not to get too near the edge. There was nothing you could do here in fact except climb down through a tangle of sharp boulders to the far end of the hole, where the water slowed and became shallow and where you could swim or fish. The Sluice Box was one of the few areas of the canyon I was fearful of: the water rushed and swirled with brutal speed, roaring loudly and making occasional sucking gulps.

Isn't it just wonderful, Mrs. Slatter called out over the din.

Peter bounced rocks over the lip of the ledge. Rosalind sat down as far from the ledge as possible. Perhaps this is one of those places you end up at, I thought, when you *lose everything*. Or not quite everything: Mrs. Slatter handed out little waxed-paper packets of gingersnaps, four each. I didn't know how to restart the conversation with Rosalind.

On our way back, Mrs. Slatter paused every now and then to give us botany lessons. I knew the plants she pointed out but not all their names, certainly not the Latin names for rabbit bush, sage, Mormon tea, various cacti, several types of willows, Shasta daisies, horsetails, clovers, alders, juniper and piñon, ponderosa pine, gooseberry, and a few species she puzzled over, snapping twigs off and dropping them in the paper sack to look up later back at the lodge. Rosalind tried to ignore this exercise even when Mrs. Slatter thrust a crushed leaf under her nose to smell; Peter, taking it as some kind of game, brought her the same specimens again and again. I was at that age when I wasn't certain what to make of adults who knew everything or almost everything and whose displays of expertise suggested a need for more exertion than I was willing to make. But plants, at least, stayed in place, unlike the butterflies another friend of the family had tried to interest me in. After a day of wild chasing with a borrowed net, I succeeded only in catching the same common species again and again. As Mrs. Slatter paused and leaned over to inspect a new plant or bush, her khaki skirt lifted in back. The long morning became suffused with the smell of sage and the vanilla-like scent of ponderosa bark, and the glow of her golden calves.

We returned to the lodge in time for lunch.

The days before the men came back down from the mine passed languorously; during the heat of the day the only signs of life at times were insects hovering in the clear air and darting in and out of the shadows of the cottonwoods. Rosalind had drawn back into her impenetrable shell. I was at best a minor annoyance, a lesser version of Peter or even at times her mother, an interrupter of her nonstop reading, a blur beyond the periphery of her blinders. If I knew somewhat more about her, it was only through overhearing Mrs. Slatter's idle confidences to Mother.

I've told Rosalind that being the best student in her class is not always the most important thing in life. You could, I've told her, spend a little more time with your friends and not hurt your grades. I've told her she could have a slumber party at the house.

Mother wanted to know what a slumber party was.

On another occasion: She even stayed home one Saturday night and wouldn't go to the movies with her friends. When will all this reading stop?

I later overheard that the silver bracelet Rosalind now wore on her right wrist had been the gift of a great-aunt, knowledge that precluded me from pretending I didn't know and asking her where it had come from. I sensed that she would have immediately detected the fib.

As I sat in the wicker chair on the veranda reading off and on I felt like one of the toads that sometimes stationed itself at night out the back door when we had left the outside light on, waiting for a moth to flutter within reach. I could almost hear the words come out of her mouth: Scotty, do you want to go for a walk? Scotty, I would like to go to the river for a swim. Scotty, when are you going to show me your secret meadow? Your ruby. Your . . . In a solicitous tone of voice I had never yet heard. But the words never came.

Peter was mostly content building structures of sticks and small rocks out in the sand of the driveway where they were certain to be run over should the Slatters ever want to move their car. I almost envied his childish contentment and self-absorption. He had apparently given up trying to torment Rosalind. Whenever I left the lodge for the river he wanted to go with me—Mrs. Slatter had told him he was too young to be in the water by himself. Once I slipped out through the back door in the afternoon and hiked upstream through the rocks to a long series of slow bends, where the banks were wide and grassy and the water shallow enough to wade all the way to the other side. But the reward of this solitude was less than I had anticipated. Since no one knew where I was, and because the place was so relatively wide and open, I couldn't think of it as an intimate hiding place like my others, the crawl space under the lodge or my meadow up on the slope above the lodge. Here I was almost beyond finding. Without a friend along, the place seemed remote and empty, too hot, the slow-moving water tepid, without the refreshing bite of the shallow spring-fed rapids at the beach. I had passed beyond that imagined fencing that enclosed the family, the group, and was alone—without the nearby presence of others, however unwanted, I had passed into an almost-absolute aloneness that tasted flat and was perhaps even tinged with fear.

I did not yet have the sense to know that Rosalind's ability to maintain her self-created shell depended on the larger embrace of others, the routines, the domestic noises and smells around her, even of those she thought she was trying to avoid. I wondered whether I would ever have even a glimmer of how I might pry my way into her hermetic world. As I walked back along the grassy bank toward the lodge I felt quite hopeless. Rosalind would leave in a few days as she always did, reading in the backseat of the Studebaker and not even looking up to say good-bye.

I slipped in through the back door and went up to my room. The lodge was quiet except for the creaking of the chains of the wicker swing in the veranda. My bunk bed offered a refuge, stuffy but enclosed, protected. Idly I played with the knot concealing my hiding place in the wall. It tipped out into my palm. I propped myself up on an elbow and peered into the dark space. Two studs at right angles formed a little shelf behind the pine paneling. The ruby was there, upside down. Beyond, in the depths, there was something else just within reach of my fingers: a strand or thread, grayish in the dim light. I was able to snag it with my index and middle fingers and slowly withdraw the mottled red-and-gray cylinder of a firecracker. I had forgotten about it. Three years before I had filched it from an open pack in Mickey's suitcase and stuffed it hurriedly into the hole. Walter had brought them back from Mexico on a business trip but had forbidden Mickey to set them off within Aunt Ruby's hearing. During their stay that summer, Mickey and I had tried to devise ways to blow them up without the adults knowing but we were never alone or far enough away from the lodge. We came close to lighting one in the ashtray of their prewar Mercury coupe with the doors closed and windows rolled up but at the last minute Walter came around the corner of the lodge in search of something in the trunk and chased us out of the car.

This one I would explode. The logic of the plan unfolded rapidly. When no one was looking I would take a couple of matches from the kitchen and disappear into the crawl space under the lodge. There was a row of small screened vents along the outside rail of the veranda, just below the level of the floor; on most of them the screen had rusted away. One of the vents was next to where Rosalind had set up her fortress, about three feet from where she sat. I could put the firecracker on the ledge of the vent, where she wouldn't see it, light it, and—well, I wasn't certain what would happen next. She would jump, scream, she would be transformed, the explosion would make her a different person. But I doubt my thoughts were as coherent as that. All I knew was that *something would happen*. At last. It didn't occur to me until later when I went to bed that I could have easily set the lodge on fire.

I established that Mother was in her room napping and Mrs. Slatter was writing letters in a folding chair facing the river on the far side of her tent, Rosalind in her fortress, Peter lying on the wicker swing, probably asleep. Since the explosion was to be just for Rosalind, I did not think through the consequences of it being almost as loud to Mrs. Slatter and Peter—again, not until much later. After picking up a few matches in the kitchen, I squeezed through the back door and went around the back of the lodge to the southeast corner of the veranda. Peter was swinging again, and the squeaking of the chains masked the scraping sounds made as I lifted the sagging hatch to the crawl space. I turned on the light to make certain the black widow hadn't moved and then turned it off again. The trench ran along under the veranda but about six feet separated it from the south wall. When I reached a position opposite the vent nearest Rosalind's fortress, the next to the last one from the end, I discovered that the space was so tight between the joists above and the powdery dirt floor I would have to crawl on my stomach over to the vent. This was not part of the plan.

Directly above me the floorboards creaked as Rosalind shifted position. I almost gave up. What if I sneezed or coughed? Or if my asthma came back? But I went ahead, brushing cobwebs out of the way. Little puffs of powdery dirt rose as I scuttled forward toward the vent. Once there, I pulled the firecracker and matches out of my shirt pocket. Up on elbows I could see a strip of the Slatter's green tent, but nothing more without bumping my head on the floorboards. I placed the firecracker on the ledge of the vent, took a deep breath, suppressed a cough, and lit the match, which seemed to make a very loud noise, and touched the flame to the fuse of twisted paper. After blowing out the match, I slid back a foot, put fingers in my ears, closed my eyes. After a moment there was a soft *ffftt* sound, then nothing. I opened my eyes to a cloud of blue smoke, sharp yet sweet smelling. A dud! Above my head I heard Rosalind's voice. After a moment the words finally came together and made sense: What's that smell? The floorboards banged and creaked as someone walked over to the screen door. I grabbed the firecracker casing and slid back into the trench and dropped down into it just as through a vent hole I glimpsed Peter peering around outside. A moment later I heard Mrs. Slatter call out, Peter, what are you doing? You're not playing with matches again, are you?

No.

There was more tramping up above my head as Mrs. Slatter came to investigate, a brief altercation between her and Peter, more footsteps, then quiet. After a while the swing started squeaking again. I sat in the shadows for a long time. I was covered in dust and cobwebs. My nose itched. My lungs hurt. I had lost track of where Mrs. Slatter had gone. Into the kitchen?

Back to her camp chair on the other side of the tent? I buried the spent firecracker and matches in the loose dirt at the bottom of the trench. I brushed myself off as best I could and struggled out of the hatch and trotted back around behind the lodge. I waited around the corner from the back door until the voices of the women had moved off, presumably to the dining room or veranda, and then walked quickly by a circuitous route to the beach, where I pulled off my dust-caked pants and flopped into the water, shirt still on, just as the afternoon thunderheads obscured the sun, and held myself under as long as I could stand it, letting the water wash away all but the agonizing memory of my failed prank.

The enormity of what could have happened hung before my eyes like the billowing cloud of smoke in the first movie I remember being taken to by Mother and Dad. I would have been four or five. In the film a barn caught fire in the middle of the night and burned to the ground. No doubt the neighborhood rallied and a new barn was raised, sparing the family financial ruin, but I was so terrified at the flaming barn—I had not yet seen a real fire—that I paid little attention to the probably happy ending. In the days following the dud firecracker, I was quieter than usual, kept to myself even more, to the point that even Mother noticed.

Are you feeling all right, Scotty?

The dinner table remark caused Rosalind to cast an almost-lingering glance in my direction.

The return of Dad and Mr. Slatter on the afternoon train the next day brought me back to myself. The men were filled with the usual mine news, which they knew would be of little interest to the women, and the women chatted about the ordinary events of the past three days. I was seized with panic at the thought that someone would bring up the *strange smell*, which would surely cause Mr. Slatter and Dad to turn their gazes on me—me, the clever one, who knew the answers to most of the little mysteries of the lodge. But the event had been forgotten. The men spent the late afternoon with drinks at the dining room table going over topographic maps and sketches of the various strata of the mine that Mr. Slatter had made over the past ten or fifteen years, and which he had brought along on this trip. When the time came to set the table for dinner, Mr. Slatter rolled up the maps and drawings and slipped them back into his canvas bag. Dad was fretful, smoking more than usual. When dinner was served, it became clear that the adults were going to have a serious conversation while they ate, even with the children present, and in defiance of Mother's rule about no talking about the mine during dinner. We assumed our usual places: Dad at the head of the table, Mother to his right, Mrs. Slatter to his left, Mr. Slatter next to Mother, an empty space opposite him. Rosalind made a dash into what was usually my place at the end of the table, book held casually almost out of sight, forcing me to sit next to her father, with Peter opposite. She had picked up enough on the mood of the evening to know that she could probably get away with reading at the table. After Mrs. Slatter and Mother passed out the plates—a sort of Spam stew made of leftovers—she slid her opened book slowly out from beneath the table cloth and opened it on her lap. This forced her to sit at a slightly awkward distance from the table. After settling in her chair, Mrs. Slatter cast a long disapproving glance at Rosalind but said nothing.

The dinner table was quiet for a few minutes as everyone began to eat. Whenever Rosalind needed to turn a page, she looked up, took a forkful of the stew, dabbed her lips with her left hand while turning the page with the right.

Hal thinks we're going to have to close down the mine completely, Dad said.

Mother and Mrs. Slatter looked up at Mr. Slatter. Flooding, he said, gas, you name it. Nothing new. It's just getting worse. How long has it been in operation, Scotty?

Since the eighteen seventies, I think. My grandfather filed the original claim.

When? Mother asked.

We could keep the smelter supplied for two months longer with what we have on hand, Dad suggested. Maybe longer.

Peter was slowing rolling a soggy canned pea across the tablecloth with the tip of his knife in Rosalind's direction, no doubt hoping it would drop over the edge of the table onto her book.

Would you stop that, Peter, she hissed.

Mr. Slatter cast an absent eye in their direction.

She's reading at the table again, Peter said.

Would you please shut up.

Children, Mrs. Slatter said. We're having a serious conversation.

Rosalind slapped her book closed but slowly reopened it.

Ruby will need to be told, Mother said. Aunt Ruby and Walter and Mickey would be arriving in around a week.

She'll be all right, Dad said. He was about to say something else but looked up and kept silent. A wall had been approached. Money was talked about only within the family, and not with children present. It was to be some years before I learned the full extent to which Aunt Ruby had bailed out Dad and Mother during the frequent difficult periods with the mine operation, with some money from investments made during earlier prosperous decades and some that she had inherited. I pretended to be deeply engaged with the soggy stew.

How exactly would bankruptcy work? Mrs. Slatter asked.

Dad looked up but was silent for a moment. The courts in this case, he said, would sell off the assets and divide the proceeds among the creditors. It wouldn't affect us personally other than . . .

None of these terms were new to me but I would have no clear sense of what they meant until many years later, when I went through the meager financial records of the era.

Rosalind gasped, raised her eyes with a startled look, turned red, and resumed eating too fast. Soon her eyes lowered again to her book.

I'm full, said Peter, throwing his head down on his elbow beside his plate.

I'm so sorry, Irma, said Mrs. Slatter. This is terrible news. Are you certain there is nothing that can be done, Hal?

Wait until a tunnel collapses and a dozen miners are trapped down there, yes, you could do that, Mr. Slatter said with his usual cheer.

Frankly it might be a relief, Mother said softly, closing it down.

One of the family secrets, or unspoken secrets, was how

many miners had been killed in accidents in the past seventy years, though in this Aunt Ruby was her usual unsentimental self. Once when she had taken me and Mickey out to a movie and dinner in Chicago and I had ordered more than I could eat, and she had primed herself with a couple of drinks, she leaned over to me and said in a low, insistent voice, I hope you know how many miners have died so you could have food on the table in front of you.

Puzzled by the statement—I was probably seven at the time—I asked innocently, as if she had posed a problem of arithmetic, How many?

She drew back, incensed at the apparent callousness of the question, which, on recollection I doubt she had asked fully aware of its radical implications. Aunt Ruby was not one to question the basic economic relations of the world: she did not doubt that we were fully entitled to our dinners and all the rest. After a moment, tight-lipped, she replied: Nine. The worst was 1918.

I had ended up finishing my meal. For a year or two afterward I assumed that every mine disaster reported in the papers and the occasional ones in movie newsreels happened at our mine, despite knowing that ours was located in Colorado, not West Virginia or Pennsylvania, and that it produced silver and other metals, not coal or iron.

We've known for a long time it's been coming, Mr. Slatter added.

Mother rose to clear the table.

Rosalind and Peter, please give Irma a hand, Mrs. Slatter said and stood up herself.

After Mother left the room, Mr. Slatter turned to Dad and said, You're sure this isn't going to put a crimp on things . . .

Dad waved a dismissive hand, which coincidentally waved away smoke from the cigarette he had just lit. My father warned me, he said. Get out when you can, he once told me. Though he never could himself. An inherited disease, I suppose.

Mrs. Slatter was stacking plates at the table. She turned and looked at me but said nothing. Perhaps she was searching for signs in me of this mysterious disease, fear of which was to haunt me for a few days until a lack of symptoms caused me to forget about it. Plates cleared, dessert was brought in: canned peaches. Rosalind and Peter sat down again and the women returned to the table. Rosalind repositioned her book on her lap, nudged her glasses down to the tip of her nose. The adults' conversation wandered off in various directions until Mrs. Slatter brought it back. Will you still come here summers? she asked.

Dad pushed his chair back and let his eyes rest on Mother. She said, I don't suppose there will be much point, will there? Would you miss it, Scotty?

Would I miss it? Dad repeated thoughtfully. He let the question hang in the air. Irma wouldn't, obviously. He craned his neck to peer around Mother and Mr. Slatter at me. What about you, Scotty Junior?

This was perhaps the first time a truly serious question, if indeed it was serious—I couldn't be sure—was asked of me. Everyone was staring at me except Rosalind, who bestowed only a quick upward flick of the eyes. It was as if I was back in school and had been asked a question by the teacher when I least expected it. What was the correct answer? I was inexperienced in loss and disappointment, at least in any direct way. I would not know until much later what a charmed childhood I had led, in large part due to summers at the lodge, where my own private experience was at odds with the official family view of the lodge and summers in the canyon as a place where Dad and Aunt Ruby had had to endure the strict regimens of unhappy and domineering parents and aunts and uncles—but to which they returned each summer since to somehow erase or exorcise those years.

What about you, Scotty Junior: Would you miss it?

No, I finally said.

When the time came to wash the dinner dishes I had finally come to the knowledge that Rosalind had won out. I had given up trying to make conversation after the first night together at the sink when she had ignored what she took to be a silly question from me—How many books have you read?—and thereafter we performed the chore in silence. Instead of breaking down her barriers, prying open her shell, I had learned from her how to strengthen and seal off my own walls and even find a degree of contentment within, and to regard most attempts to get messages through as impositions on my carefully arranged privacy. I could tell that Mrs. Slatter regarded this development with both curiosity and solicitude. I could get out the Parcheesi board, she hinted several times to our backs while we stood at the sink, the response to which was an irritable *No, Mother, I have to read*. Once, out of politeness, I consented to play with Peter and the two women while the men were up at the mine. Peter chafed at the rules and tried to change them, and Mother played with her usual lassitude while nursing a glass of sherry.

This state of affairs did not so much quiet the inner tumult Rosalind's presence fueled as project it into my reading, into a sealed-off space where I could allow my emotions to rage while maintaining a perfectly impassive exterior—or so at least I hoped. The sensations I was harboring were so powerful, yet so imperfectly understood, that I was not entirely certain I was managing to contain them within myself. Fortunately there was no one at the lodge with the sharpness of vision or keenness of ear of Aunt Ruby to unmask me, and I walked around, sat reading on the veranda, sat with the others at meals, tremulous with a sense of ripeness; I feared the slightest gesture or most trivial word would cause me to burst open in a flood of tears or hysterical laughter—or I wasn't certain what. While washing the dishes I became fearful of carving knives and marveled at how little, almost nothing, stood between me and the act of plunging the soapy blade into Rosalind's breast or her mother's back. About that time I became obsessed with the granular. Crumbs on the table, dust, unrecognizable bits of organic matter on windowsills, sand, gravel, the coalesced matter of stones, flecks, chips, tiny broken bits of anything. At the river, this became soothing when I could tear myself away from the latest Trollope and sneak down to the beach by myself and lay on my boulder and peer into the water at eddies of small gravel and swirling bits of dark decaying wood and bark, and on the sand amid clumps of grass where I would follow the progress of foraging ants and tiny spiders through their minute but complicated landscapes. It was perhaps the randomness that absorbed me, the impossibility of pattern, a reading of marks that could never yield meaning beyond the endless vast sum of it all.

After a stroll down to the beach after dinner in the waning

light while Rosalind and I read on the veranda, the adults returned and settled themselves in the living room over port and
brandy. By the time I went up to my room they were all in a
merry mood such as I had never known, and as I lay in my bunk
upstairs reading the cackling laughter and whoops of joy occasionally broke through my concentration. I read late. When I
finally turned out the light I lay for what seemed like hours in
a state of overheated expectation in which the bunting of some
vague future billowed in the wind and people were rushing this
way and that, and I was following, now by car, now by train,
toward a destination I knew I was certain I would attain. The
room was hot. I got up and opened the window wider. The slow
even wash of the river muffled the voices echoing up the stairs.
I climbed back up into my bunk and fell into a deep sleep.

When the Slatters left two days later I took malicious pleasure in reading on the veranda. Now and then I raised my eyes
to watch Rosalind, with the ill humor of one awakened from a
dream I could still bask in, pack her suitcase and carry things
down to the trailer. Her irritability earned constant sharp re-
proaches from Mrs. Slatter and even inspired bossiness in Peter
as he danced around her, correcting her aggressive sloppiness.
That doesn't go there, stupid, he kept calling out. As Rosalind
stalked back and forth between the veranda and the trailer,
tight-lipped, nose in the air, Mr. Slatter would look up and
exchange glances and eye rolls with his wife, in between checking oil and water under the hood, tire pressures, the trailer
hitch, safety chain, electrical connections to the trailer taillights. Everything packed, he cinched tight the orange canvas
tarp over the top of the trailer. Mrs. Slatter closed the tailgate
grub box and latched it closed. When Mr. Slatter carried their

metal ice chest out to the trunk of the car, this was the signal that they were about to leave. Mother and Dad joined them in the driveway. I tried to get by with an abstracted wave from the wicker swing in the veranda, but Mother called out, Scotty, please come down and say good-bye to the Slatters.

Rosalind was pouting in the backseat, not even reading. Beside her Peter was bouncing up and down. Bye, she said to the back of the front seat. Mr. Slatter started the engine, climbed back out. The adults shook hands stiffly. The Slatters climbed back in and Mr. Slatter swung the car through the turnaround and they headed to the back of the lodge toward the driveway up the hill. We could hear Mr. Slatter gunning the engine, trailer hitch banging, tires skidding. Partway up the hill the car stopped. We heard doors slamming. When we walked hurriedly around the lodge it became clear that the steep road, badly rutted from recent rains, had defeated Mr. Slatter's attempt to maintain enough speed to reach the crest at the railroad tracks above. Dad had talked of having Mr. Smedley bring a load of crushed rock up from Basalt Junction to fill in the ruts but had never gotten around to it. By the time we reached them, Mr. Slatter had already positioned his wife and children to push the rear of the trailer. Dad and I joined them, leaving Mother at the bottom of the hill, and I took up a position next to Rosalind. Mr. Slatter stuck his head out the driver's window and restarted the engine. Okay, he shouted, let's go.

The car and trailer rolled back a couple of inches as he let out the clutch. With a series of shudders it began advancing up the hill at a creeping pace, rear wheels spinning and shooting out a spray of sand and gravel. Finally the trailer began to lurch out of our grasp. Rosalind let out a quick little scream. She had snagged her bracelet on one of the hooks that held down the tarp cord. It was made out of silver links in the form of little roses. I jumped around her and freed it just as the trailer leapt away. We stumbled and fell to our knees as car and trailer fishtailed their way up the rest of the grade. I pushed really hard! Peter shouted.

We were all winded. Rosalind said nothing. But she looked at me longer than she ever had before. We hiked up the hill to rejoin Mr. Slatter. The adults laughed and said good-bye again, Mother waving from the bottom of the hill. The Slatters climbed back into the Studebaker.

Looking halfway in my direction out the window, Rosalind said, Good-bye, Scotty.

It was the first time I heard her utter my name.

Five

THERE WAS THE usual uncertainty about the arrival of Aunt
Ruby, Walter, and Mickey. Punctilious in most other things,
Aunt Ruby assumed that the reasons for her erratic arrivals
were transparent to others even at a distance, perhaps under
the sweeping supposition, *They'll understand*. The remoteness
of the lodge presumed the intervention of the unpredictable,
and perhaps what was unusual was Mother and Dad's never-
corrected expectation that visitors traveling by car would ar
rive within an hour or so of the time they had decided on, with
no allowance for flat tires, overheating engines, wrong turns,
bad weather, rockslides. The relative regularity of the train
may have been to blame here.

Days passed. Maybe they've decided not to come after all,
Mother suggested wistfully, no doubt hoping that a change in
their plans would provide an excuse to go back to Denver a
week or two early. My quiet days down at the river were strung

taut with an anticipation not entirely connected with their approaching arrival. I couldn't put a name to it, this new impatience. Rosalind's words hung in my memory with a warm sense of unbridled promise but I hadn't the slightest idea of how to bridge the distance that was lengthening each day to well over a thousand miles. Sometimes, weary at reading, I would lay down the book and climb up on my boulder out in the water and stare fiercely at the apron of basalt boulders across the river and up at the fissured crags that rose vertically to the sky to the west. I would squeeze my will into focus. *Make something happen!* Something other than the rustling swirl of water teasing my bare feet, something other than pinpricks of sensation that dotted my skin in the hot sun, the sound of my own breathing, the scratching noise of the cloth of my trunks against the rough patches of the boulder, the hum of insects. *Anything!* If I stared with enough concentration at a crack high up on the cliff, just to the right of a thin white waterfall of droppings from the bald eagle nest, if I directed all the force of my being into it, then it would split apart wider and come crashing down in a rolling tumult of deep booms and clouds of dust.

After a time my tailbone would begin to ache and I would slip off the rock into the cooling water and paddle awhile, dip my head under, emerge back into the sun and air with everything blurred and somehow distant again. These moments came once or twice a day, usually but not always accompanied by an erection, which I regarded as an unwanted distraction. *Go away!* But it only stiffened, threatening to stay with me so long that I began to worry how to walk back to the lodge without it being evident. I feared I would never become used to the insistent companionship of this other being, this clinging creature I had until now thought of as part of a passing phase. How many times had I peed in the past without paying the slightest attention to it? Now when I unzipped my pants or pulled down my trunks, there it was, suddenly expanding to my touch, as if to say like a cloyingly familiar relative, *Where have you been?* or *What took you so long?* Each morning I woke up worried that it had grown even larger in the night. Would it ever stop?

Reading eventually offered solace, deflation, as I lay on the thing in the sand. *The thing.* I had as yet no word for it, though by that age certainly I had heard them all and had seen most of them scratched into walls above urinals. Nor did I think it odd that in the dozen novels and story collections I pulled at random and read through from the sagging wooden shelves of the alcove below the stairs—the "library"—I had found no direct allusion or description of anyone's *things*, men's or women's. It was clear that something had gotten out of control, and that I might be the only one who suffered from this condition.

I passed the days between Rosalind's departure and the others' arrival wrestling to control myself, finding moments of tranquility in the more exciting and often-violent passages of the novels I was reading—though other episodes of a romantic nature would trigger a relapse and at mealtimes, sitting around the table with Dad and Mother, whose presence had the effect of making the thing shrivel down to its former usual size. They probably wondered why I hung around them so long after dinner as they rambled on about some article one of them had read in one of the old magazines they had brought to the lodge, the *Saturday Evening Post, Colliers, Look, TIME,* or letters that Mr. Sanchez had handed down from the morning train, along with the occasional two-day-old *Denver Post.*

When will you close it down? Mother asked during a pause in her knitting.

Dad lowered the newspaper and stared out into the deep crystalline blue of the last light through the veranda screens. He shook the paper and resumed reading. Then he lowered it again. We'll see what Ruby says, he answered. He had been back to the mine only once, and only for a night, since the Slatter's visit.

This held no interest for me. The future was a blinding white cloud in which all possibilities were diffused. Everything would be different despite the daily evidence to the contrary, in the leisurely yet somehow rigid routine of each day, from the moment the morning sun pried its way through the crack under my door and the rising heat in the upstairs drove me from the flannel sleeping bag and its rich exhalations of bodily fragrances, through the predictable steps of breakfast, the still-cold sand of the beach spraying over bare feet in the morning, the rising heat of the afternoon, the midafternoon thunderheads that occasionally delivered brief showers and rarer downpours, the slow fall into darkness. The monotony was relieved by the weekly drive down to Basalt Junction, where the revolving wire paperback rack had fewer titles with each visit. Time did not move, however much I willed it; I was trapped inside an aquarium or a block of ice. Outside, beyond some distant surface, or up high, or down below, where the narrow-gauge tracks ended, or where they connected with standard-gauge lines, which in turn connected up with the transcontinental lines to the West Coast and to Chicago and the East and even up into Canada and down into Mexico, life teemed and tumbled. From the beach I followed the sound of the daily trains as they faded into the distance, up the canyon wall in the morning, down into the depths of the canyon later in the afternoon, clinging to the last faint clank or the echo of the whistle as to a cord or rope that might somehow, at the last moment, yank me out of this stillness and transport me far away at last. I regretted that I hadn't brought up to the lodge a box of illustrated travel brochures I had accumulated from back-of-the-magazine advertisements, for the cities and counties of England and Scotland and the tourist regions of France, with images of those villages and cathedrals and castles and city streets that had emerged unscathed from the war—the first postwar attempts to attract American tourists back to Europe. I had been astounded at how the coupons requesting information, which I had timidly filled out, had yielded so many fat envelopes of brochures. Mother was suspicious but said nothing. Lacking the actual folders at the lodge I re-created and no doubt embellished them in memory, the dense maps, the empty country lanes, the tame smooth rivers, the canals, the white beaches, and the metallic maroon three-speed English bike on which I would ride through these landscapes alone—alone because the exertion of placing another, a Rosalind, in the picture was too great, too complicated. I had no sense of how I would pay for the adventure, how I would eat, where I would sleep, or even how I would cross the Atlantic, though I was certain that as soon as I returned to Denver, brochures would offer solutions for all those problems. I had begun to notice magazine advertisements for the Cunard Line, the French Line, the Holland-American Line, United States Lines, and knew that as soon as I was back home I would be sending for more brochures illustrating the mysteries of the *Queen Mary* and *La Liberté*.

I had no sense yet that these summers at the lodge could be

seen as exotic in any way, despite the Nesbitts' initial enthusiasm and later discomfort during their brief time here. That would come later, in college, where Midwesterners and Easterners would be thrown together with a handful of Westerners, among whom I was grouped despite having spent my early childhood in Chicago, where we would begin to peer into the lives different from our own, other families, other ways of saying things, eating, dressing, and where I began to have an inkling that this landscape, which had so strongly imprinted itself on my psyche, was in many respects unimaginable to others. In college I began to catch glimpses of it through new eyes, in the responses to my vague allusions to my childhood summers, which emerged in casual remarks and banter during late-night bull sessions in the dorm. And in one of those odd switchbacks of life, Frankie Nesbitt, transformed into a thin, thoughtful man, became a close friend for a time in our early thirties. But in this seemingly eternal meantime at the lodge I was stuck within an unalterable daily rhythm, trapped at the bottom of a deep canyon, its steep black walls having become an insurmountable barrier to entering the rest of the world, and without the words yet to break the spell of this imprisonment. I read and read, or rather stared intently at the pages as they flew past, deep into the blurry tunnels that led to these other worlds, Trollope's and Tolstoy's flowing sentences accompanied by fleeting images from the British Tourist Office brochures. When my eyes or body finally wearied, or I was interrupted, the boulders and the river and trees and stone walls of the lodge rushed back at me, regaining their enclosing solidity, clamping me back into the present moment. Only in the sound of water swishing past, cottonwood leaves brushing against each other in the breeze, the clicking of insects, chirping of birds, the occasional splash of a rising trout, only here was there a hint that something, somehow, might change.

Several days, perhaps even a week, into this state of comfortable claustrophobia, Aunt Ruby and Walter, who was never to earn an honorific "Uncle," and Cousin Mickey arrived in a dusty but brand-new metallic-green Buick Roadmaster sedan with Hydra-Matic Drive. Mouth agape I stared, as they climbed out shouting greetings, at the machine and its enormous chrome grill, which suggested a slightly bored, probably malevolent, monster. Mickey had grown. He had also begun to shave. A wash of fine dark stubble extended halfway down his jaw, and a sharp line ended his sideburns. Last spring I took notice of these changes in some of my male schoolmates, who had begun to sprout hairs unevenly on their faces, and whether they ignored them or cut or shaved them off, and I was apprehensive of this advent on my own face. I particularly dreaded the whole business of having to walk into the local drugstore and pick out a razor and blades under the too-watchful eye of Mr. Luby, the druggist, and wonder whether he would exchange meaningful glances with Mrs. Luby while I was still there or only after I had left. I had taken to studying magazine advertisements for clues about how to negotiate this new labyrinth, but they addressed only the entirely different problems of grown men with heavy beards.

I had just put on my trunks to go down to the river. Aunt Ruby sized me up: Brown as a nut but still feeding that tapeworm, I see. She turned to Mother, who was standing at the foot of the steps with a dish towel in hand. All he needs is filling up with hamburgers. Irma, how lovely to see you.

Walter squeezed my hand as hard as he could and grunted.

It's hot, Mickey said, flapping the front of his shirt in and out for ventilation.

You've come at the right time, Dad said to Ruby as she gave him a peck on the cheek.

Yes, the news was in the paper this morning. You must have heard from the railroad people. Her tone was both arch and irritable.

What news? Dad asked.

Oh, you haven't? She turned to Walter. Did you bring the paper?

What paper?

I asked you to. I am quite certain I asked you to bring the paper along, Walter. She turned back to Dad. He never listens to me. He can't hear the higher tones, you know, like dogs, or whatever. Mickey, you can take the cases upstairs.

What news? Dad asked again.

Well, they've finally got around to it, Aunt Ruby said. They've filed for abandonment. The whole narrow-gauge section or whatever you call it. Nobody told you?

I suppose that settles it, Dad mused. Slatter says we have to close down the mine.

Mickey had opened the trunk of the Buick but was standing and listening. Mother was folding up the dish towel. Ruby looked at Dad thoughtfully. Count your blessings, she said. Then she turned. Mickey, would you please take the luggage upstairs. And what about you, Scotty Junior?

Walter grunted. Mickey fussed around in the back of the car and pulled out the leather suitcases one by one and placed them on the ground.

Flooding, collapse, Dad was saying, explosions from gas.

It's all possible. We've exhausted everything that's accessible. And now without the railroad . . .

Perhaps we should go inside and have something refreshing, Aunt Ruby said. You at least brought the gin, didn't you, Walter?

That I did.

In an English novel I had recently read there had been a lot of gin drinking. I was excited at the thought of seeing the actual liquid, the effects on the adults. Lugging suitcases, Mickey and I followed the adults into the lodge by way of the veranda and then dragged the cases upstairs. When we came back down, Walter was in the kitchen mixing drinks from a clear bottle of gin and a green bottle of Vermouth. Mickey and I returned to the doorway between the living room and the veranda.

I've already written Courtland, Dad was saying, to ask him to draw up the bankruptcy papers.

What's that? Mickey whispered in my ear.

Tell you later, I whispered back.

I wonder, said Dad. Would Grandfather have guessed it would end like this?

It usually does, Aunt Ruby observed.

Walter arrived with the drinks. No ice, of course, he said.

It will be a relief of sorts, you know, Ruby, Dad said, raising his glass.

Well, then, to relief, Aunt Ruby toasted. To relief, relief, and yet more relief. She laughed. Have you actually talked to Courtland about this? Boys, have you finished with the suitcases?

Mickey and I went back outside. What's bankruptcy? he asked.

It's when you go out of business, I think.

Oh.

We grabbed the last of the large suitcases and carried them upstairs. On our return trip we paused again at the doorway to the veranda. Dad and Walter had stepped away from the women and Dad was explaining something.

I never feel well up here, Mother said to Aunt Ruby.

But do you feel well anywhere, Irma? Aunt Ruby shot back, then looked down into her glass with pursed lips. I'm sorry, that was uncalled for. What does your doctor think, that new one you've been going to?

He wants me to have another—

Boys, are you finished yet? If not, get on with it. If so, go down to the river or find something to do. Please. Aunt Ruby gave us both severe looks.

We unloaded the rest of the trunk and carried the things upstairs without pausing at the veranda door this time. I was already in my swimming trunks. Mickey fished his out of his suitcase and I stepped out in the hallway while he put on them on. We headed down to the river. There would be another hour or two of sun before the afternoon thunderheads gathered.

They're sending me to school in Switzerland, Mickey announced as we stood on the edge of the water. In October.

Switzerland. Images from the brochures flared into vividness. Cogwheel railways. Cyclists pausing to breathe in the air of the vast panoramas. The white cross on the red flag.

Private school, he continued. They want me to learn a bunch of languages. And all kinds of crap. Shit.

The word stung my ears.

Think they can see us from here? he said, turning around to

glance back at the cottonwoods that more or less screened the beach from the veranda. He unwrapped his towel to reveal a pack of Camels and a book of matches. I beckoned toward my boulder and a couple of other large rocks, behind which we wouldn't be seen. We sloshed over and ducked down. Here, have one. He tore open the silver end of the pack and pulled up a cigarette.

Maybe later, I muttered.

He grabbed a cigarette with his lips and somewhat awkwardly pulled off a match and struck it, lighting the tip. The match hit the water with a hiss. Then he rolled the cigarettes and matchbook up into his towel and placed it on a flat rock sticking out of the water. He sucked deeply and coughed.

Walter will kill me if he finds out.

Cigarette in his lips, he stood up and peered over the top of the boulder and then slipped his thumbs beneath the elastic of his trunks and pulled them down and off. Hey, come on, he said, take it off. Nobody can see.

Timidly I stood up and slipped off my trunks and plopped back down in the water just as the thing began to swell. I lay back in the slow current while Mickey sat on a rock, half-submerged, smoking.

There's this girl in my class, he said. Marlene.

He was staring into space across the river, at a tumble of lichen-spotted boulders. I was soon to discover that Mickey seemed to be carrying on a voluble inner monologue that now and then surfaced into speech, apropos of nothing in particular, whether I responded or not.

Marlene. She's just right for me. Blond or not quite blond, blue eyes, you know.

He puffed in silence, made several attempts to blow out smoke rings, or so I guessed. When the butt was down to an inch, he flicked it in a wide arc downriver, where it hit the water, spun, disappeared. I lay quietly in the water, wondering how I would ever be able to get out. Mickey, who was about ten feet away, stood up, peered over the boulder. His, too, was fully erect. He looked down at it, made it waggle back and forth, smiled slyly in my direction, sat down in the water and laid back. The tip of his penis broke through the water for a moment as if to have a look, then disappeared.

Ross, he said. Marlene Ross. Goddamn. How's that for a name? She's pretty smart, too.

I began shivering uncontrollably, less from the cold than the sheer excitement of all that was new, our nakedness, the smell of tobacco still lingering in the air, or at least in my imagination. I stood up and quickly wrapped a towel around my waist, leaned against the warm boulder. Mickey ignored my perfunctory questions uttered through chattering teeth. He bobbed up and down in the water, threw his head back under the surface, brought it back up, shook the water out of his short hair, not quite blond, like, I presumed, this Marlene's. His skin was a shade darker than mine. The adults would say of him that he was *maturing*. A year older than me he looked less the boy and more the young man. There was something fixed and distracted in his bearing, perhaps the effect, I would later guess, of having been called *handsome* or *striking* by enough different people for the compliment to be believable. He sometimes resembles his father, Aunt Ruby had once said. Mickey was his nickname. His real name was Martin. Perhaps they were going to send Mickey to Switzerland in the hope that he would come back as Martin.

He thrust himself up out of the water and perched on the rock next to his towel. He unwrapped it and pulled out another cigarette, waving it in my direction. You sure?

I nodded no. He was still erect, as was I. But I had stopped shivering and was beginning to feel a warm glow reaching out to the other extremities of my body under the hot sun. A slight breeze pulsated up and down the river, a puff here and there, and the sky was still bright and clear overhead, though the afternoon thunderheads were edging over the ridge east of the canyon. At various times I had wondered whether, after all, maybe I was not the only one suffering from this affliction, and I still remembered the one time on the train I imagined that everyone, men at least, endured the experience, but here at last was a demonstration that I was not alone. Mickey was confident in his nakedness, unembarrassed by his erection, his new wisps of body hair. I realized not at the moment but later in reflection that once my shivering subsided I wanted the afternoon to go on and on, never end, with us lying about in the sun, taking dips, Mickey smoking and conjuring up visions of the girl, covering and uncovering ourselves with our towels. I slid back into the water. The shivering did not come back.

Marlene Ross. Her father owns a big brand-new Lincoln. You should see their garage.

We stayed at the river through two more cigarettes. Black clouds unfurled over the canyon and blotted out the sun. We stood up, pulled our trunks back on, waded back to the beach. The cottonwoods swayed back and forth under a strong wind now racing down the canyon. After much thunder and lightning, only a light rain fell, after which Walter ordered us to wash the Buick with wadded-up old dish towels. Mickey ate dinner with his usual absent gaze, often answering the adults' questions and requests with an irritable *What did you say?* The adults talked off and on about the mine, decided to send a telegram tomorrow to Courtland in Chicago from Basalt Junction, asking him to proceed with bankruptcy proceedings. He managed the family finances—ineptly, I eventually learned—and took care of legal matters for the mine. Aunt Ruby now and then digressed from the wandering deliberations to cast sharp glances at Mickey and me, both slouching in our chairs. Sit up, both of you. What's the matter with you boys tonight? Everyone went to bed early. Mickey tossed and turned in the upper bunk while below I was quieter but equally restless, dozing off repeatedly to images of Mickey's Marlene and the gleaming breast-like chrome protuberances of the front bumpers of the imagined Lincoln, the aroma of Mickey's illicit cigarettes, then waking up to a place that was no longer recognizably the lodge, a place where the colors and shapes had imperceptibly changed, and to which a vast new dimension had been added—to which a small patch of something caked on the crotch of my pajama bottoms was an irrelevant puzzle.

Next morning Dad and Walter decided to drive the LaSalle down to Basalt Junction to send a telegram to Courtland, and without it being discussed it was assumed that Mickey and I would go with them. We left just after breakfast. Mickey and I sat in back. Dad was dressed in the threadbare brown suit he favored while at the lodge, and Walter carried a rumpled navy-blue blazer, which he threw over the back of the seat. Freed of Aunt Ruby's exacting standards of conversation, Walter rambled on about fishing and sports, which Dad had little interest in, and the new car models announced for the fall, Howard Hughes's new Constellation airliner, the sad state of postwar passenger-rail service. They both smoked as Dad drove. The gestures of lighting their cigarettes with the car lighter, inhaling and exhaling, seemed to have more in common than their fitful phrases and unfinished sentences. Walter had served in the Pacific in the last years of the war but had not seen combat. Normally when alone with Dad he would trot out stories about the fate of inconvenient surpluses of food rations and Jeeps and walkie-talkies and landing craft and their unceremonious disposal or disappearance in the jungles of or in the waters off some tropical island. He told these tales with the smirking pride of someone who had got away scot-free with a monumental prank. I can just see some general sitting at his desk somewhere, he once said, trying to make the numbers add up. Ha!

At the gas pumps at Smedley's we climbed out of the car. Mickey pulled me aside.

Think he'll sell me some cigarettes? he asked, nodding in the direction of Mr. Smedley.

Try, I suggested. But Mrs. Smedley was presiding over the counter, a huge forbidding presence wrapped in the usual splotchy gray apron, and Walter soon positioned himself at the nearby magazine rack to thumb through the out-of-date issues of hunting and fishing and "true adventure" magazines. From what I could see, he lingered over the ambiguous advertisements inside the back covers for "fully illustrated" comic books, "party slides," and the like, which I myself had often puzzled over.

There were, as usual now, no new paperbacks. While Mr. Smedley gassed up the car and checked the oil and tires, Dad walked across the road and disappeared into the train station.

I stepped back outside. Mickey joined me. Shit, he said, shit. What is this place, anyway? A rhetorical question, since he had been to Basalt Junction almost as many times as I had. Mr. Smedley closed the hood and walked into the store and came back with a box of groceries, which he placed in the trunk. A red-and-white carton of Lucky Strikes for Dad was sticking up out of a corner of the cardboard box. Dad's smoking had never made me want to take up the habit, though I watched carefully how he handled his cigarettes, how he tapped them, inserted them between his lips, how he lit them with the match, how he delicately picked off bits of tobacco from his tongue, his way of inhaling and exhaling, the circular twist with which he extinguished the butt in the ashtray stand beside his armchair on those occasions when he didn't flick it into the fireplace. Nor did Mickey's smoking make me want to take it up either; rather, it alerted me to the possibility of defiance, though as yet without any sense of urgency or necessity. One way or another Mickey had always been a hell-raiser, as the adults would say, while my efforts in that direction had always been accidental or unintentional. Grown-ups thought of me as a *good kid*, an illusion I was content to let them enjoy, even as I knew better. In Mickey's shadow I could keep my reputation and savor risk at the same time. And study what I later saw as a developing sexual allure that I was years away from sensing in myself.

Mr. Smedley waylaid Walter on the way back to the car and regaled him, or so I guessed, with the same dirty jokes Dad had often complained of, while the rest of us waited in the car. At each of the punch lines, Walter cackled and slapped Mr. Smedley on the back. When Walter finally rejoined us, he turned to Dad with a leering smile and said, Did you hear the one about—?

More times than I can count, Dad said. Walter turned around at Mickey and me and winked.

We drove back in silence, passing the northbound morning train just as it was entering the canyon. Dad decided to park the LaSalle at the top of the drive on a sloping wide spot about ten yards away from the railroad tracks. It had been a dry summer so far, which often meant that the late rains could be intense. He and Walter were going to take the train up to the mine tomorrow, and Dad thought it prudent to leave at least one of the cars up on the road in case the driveway became impassible, should the women need to get down to Basalt Junction. Walter ordered Mickey to carry the box of groceries down the hill. The top end of the carton of Lucky Strikes bounced up and down just below his nose. After lunch Mickey and I retreated to the river and our hiding place behind the boulder, where we pulled off our trunks and sat down in the water. Mickey didn't offer me a cigarette this time, and smoked only one. He was running low.

Marlene, he mused, she was at this dance class they invited me to. I even got to dance with her once. But they didn't invite me back, idiots. I could even feel the straps of her bra. They probably thought I was too close to her, idiots.

Who?

The mothers. The chaperones. Like we were puppets or something.

I could see Mickey acting up in that kind of situation, making jokes, impolite noises. His Marlene had begun to assume some of Rosalind's features, her somewhat otherworldly look, bra straps showing faintly though the stiff material of a white blouse.

The afternoon drifted by. We lay in the water, splashed, paddled, climbed up on rocks, sunbathed, watched our own erections come and go. Two more afternoons passed in this manner. Mickey ran out of cigarettes.

Scotty, where does your dad keep his smokes?

I don't know.

Well, could you find out?

He probably took them with him up to the mine.

Not the whole carton, I bet.

He kept them in their bedroom, a place I had stopped surreptitiously exploring when I was about seven. At the time I had the good sense not to play with the huge pearl-handled .45 that lay behind a concealing bank of neatly folded handkerchiefs in a drawer high up in their wardrobe, and I was years away from understanding what the three or four thin rubber disks with thick rolled edges were, in a nightstand drawer. But I no longer felt comfortable in there. And Mother made it clear that it was her private refuge, to the point of often locking the door when she didn't want to be disturbed.

The insistence of Mickey's request became irritating. The sun seemed too hot—or I was becoming aware of sunburned patches on my rump.

Steal some from Aunt Ruby, I said.

She'd kill me.

He was probably right. She had begun to turn her attention to our long afternoon absences.

What are you boys doing all afternoon down at the river? she asked more than once over dinner.

Reading, I lied. I didn't even take a book down to the river with me. In the course of becoming conscious of my body, of possessing a body that had a life of its own beyond propulsion, digestion, and sleep, I found it difficult to concentrate on reading. Morning hours would pass with me sitting on the veranda swing, book in my lap concealing the off-again-on-again swelling beneath. I would manage to get through a page or two at most. It was worse when I dragged a camp chair out into the sun to escape the chill of early morning.

If you two get any browner we'll have to send you back to Africa, both of you.

When the men came back from the mine, Mickey hung around Walter waiting to catch him alone so he could bum a cigarette. Eventually he received a windfall in the form of three somewhat rumpled cigarettes in a half-wadded-up pack. They provided the occasion for what turned out to be our last afternoon together down at the river behind the boulder. When he had finished smoking the last, he opened up the empty packet, lay back in the water, and inserted it over his erect penis, contemplating it for a time before letting it float away downstream.

I've got Marlene's phone number but haven't called her yet. Do you think I should, Scotty?

Our nudist afternoons at the river were ended less by a temporary dearth of cigarettes than by the water having turned a heavy greenish gray overnight. We later learned that a downpour had washed out the banks of one of the tailing ponds up at the mine and sluiced the sludge down a gully into a tributary of the river. I didn't need to be told that it would be unwise to swim or even wade. Dead rainbow and brown trout, floating belly up along the edges, were sign enough. Nor was this the first time: a few years back the water had been fouled for two weeks running.

The beach offered no concealment for Mickey's smoking or anything else, and because we could no longer cool off in the river, we had to sit in the shade. Reluctantly I went back to reading, while Mickey lay on the sand, dozed, doodled with sticks, threw rocks, earnestly picked at various parts of his long well-tanned limbs in search of imperfections. His Marlene musings were becoming repetitive, lacking the stimulus of renewed experience; these alternated with fulminations against Aunt Ruby's plans to send him to private school near Geneva, thoughts on how to butter up Walter for more cigarettes without, however, becoming his *little personal slave*. Occasionally he would flick sticks or pebbles in my direction, trying to land them on the page. Oh, sorry, he would say whenever he scored a direct hit. But absently. He wasn't seeking conversation, only attention. By then I knew perfectly well that I was his sounding board, not someone whose thoughts and feelings were of any interest.

Late-afternoon thunderstorms had been hitting everywhere nearby except our part of the canyon for a week now. Finally a brief cloudburst struck just after dark. It was accompanied by raucous lightning strikes that reached down into the canyon, one close to the lodge, and it sent us running from room to room to close windows and to the kitchen cupboards for candles and lanterns. But other than a brief flicker, the electricity stayed on. The lightning strike closest to the lodge, or rather the sound it made, was odd: after the window-rattling *crack* there was a series of metallic rumbles. Echoes, we all thought, of thunder rolling up and down the canyon. The storm left as fast as it arrived, leaving the patter of water dripping from the eaves. Distant booms of thunder became fainter and fainter as the storm made its way across the mesa to the west. Breezes wafting in through the re-opened windows smelled of sage—and something sharper, acidic, which I took to be emanations from the fouled river.

The next morning, Walter was the first to sense something was wrong. He had stepped outside to smoke while the table was being set for breakfast. He came back inside.

Scotty, he said to Dad in the kitchen, why would there be a smell of gasoline outside?

I hope the car is all right, Mother commented from the range.

Probably just that new Buick of ours, said Aunt Ruby without looking up from the pancake mix she was stirring. That brand-new Buick. It's been a lemon since the day Walter brought it home from the factory, hasn't it, Walter?

I had gotten up early, excited as ever to see what changes the storm might have wrought down at the river, hoping that somehow it might have cleared up the water, though I had heard no signs of flooding during the night. The river was running higher, its color a little closer to the usual muddiness after a storm. Mickey was still in bed. I followed the men through the veranda and down the steps. The smell seemed to be coming from an almost-impenetrable thicket of squawberry bush and cottonwood saplings some ways downriver from the lodge, at the base of a tumble of boulders that led, by giant steps, up to the railway roadbed a hundred feet above.

Let's see what we can see from above, Dad suggested. We headed around the lodge and up the driveway, which was awash with new little gullies and rivulets of sand and silt. When we reached the crest, everything suddenly became clear. In the place of our tan LaSalle there stood a huge basalt boulder almost the size of the car itself. Then we saw the bent rails, the split ties, the trough the boulder had gouged out as it had slid across the tracks to its resting place. Breathless from the climb, we raced over to the edge of the drop and looked over. A trail of broken glass and bits of chrome pointed down to the rust-brown shapes of the underside of the car, partly concealed by the brush it nestled within, only one of the tires visible.

Well, I'll be . . . Walter gasped.

Huh, Dad said, then coughed. After a few moments he added, Well, I guess that's that.

Yeah, sure is.

I raced back down the hill, shouted out the headline to the women as I ran through the kitchen and upstairs to wake up Mickey.

Hey, the LaSalle went over the cliff.

What did you say? he said, sitting straight up in bed.

You heard me. Come on, come look.

The women suspended breakfast preparations and rushed out the back door. Mickey, barefoot in swimming trunks and pajama top, crept up the gravelly hill after us but eventually overtook Mother, who paused every now and then to catch her breath. At the top we all gathered to peer over the edge.

Is that it? That can't be it, Ruby exclaimed.

What do you think it is, a Sherman tank? Mickey shot back, then began hopping up and down on one foot and twisting around to look at the sole of the other. Goddamn stickers!

Watch your language, young man.

Mother had an oddly pleased expression on her face, as if to say, *At last, something terrible has happened.* It was decided that we would go back down the hill and that while the women worked on preparing breakfast we would try to get through the brush to see how badly the LaSalle was damaged, as if there was still any doubt. Down below, I pushed a tunnel through the squawberry bushes right up to the car, whose roof had been smashed in, doors crumpled and splayed open. Inside there was a jumble of seat cushions ripped loose. Gasoline was still dripping from the gas cap. When I came out, the men burrowed in one at a time.

Well, that's certainly that, Dad said.

Time for a new one, Scotty. This one doesn't have too many miles left on it, Walter observed with a guffaw.

For years afterward the wreck of the LaSalle occupied an outsized position in my memory. Upon returning to the kitchen for breakfast I was so hungry from running up and down the hill twice on an empty stomach that I fainted on the kitchen linoleum, an event Mother and Aunt Ruby attributed to distress at the destruction of the aging vehicle. I was fond of the LaSalle because I knew it so well as a backseat driver and because I was looking forward to having my first proper driving lessons behind its large steering wheel, most of whose cream-colored paint had worn off. The wreck was a real, tangible event. I was able to convince myself that the strange bangs following the thunderclap were those of the car tumbling down over the rocks. Long afterward I could recall the smell of leaking gasoline and motor oil, the odors of the tires heating up in the morning sun. In the short time before we left the lodge, I climbed the hill twice and sat on the edge of the cliff and stared down at the rusty under-carriage of the upside-down car nestled in the bushes. By comparison the closing of the mine, the bankruptcy proceedings, the eventual liquidation of the assets were remote, abstract events, nothing I chose to pay attention to at the time, though a rise in the price of silver made this in fact quite profitable for Dad and Aunt Ruby, leading to a time of family prosperity that propelled me through college and beyond. Likewise for the abandonment of much of the Denver & Rio Grande Western narrow-gauge railway network, which assumed for me only the status of a rumor, not a fact of business and history.

It was decided that we would all leave the lodge together the day after the wreck in Walter and Aunt Ruby's unreliable Buick, with minimal luggage. With six of us in the car, Aunt Ruby up front between the two men, and Mother in back between Mickey and me, the sagging Buick barely made it to the top of the driveway, scraping and banging as it went. At the top a railroad section crew was repairing the track—steel rails that probably the same crew would be removing altogether within a few months. The drive back to Denver was hot, even with all the windows down. We had to stop three or four times to let the engine cool off. A few days after returning to Denver, Dad borrowed an International pickup from Mr. Nesbitt and drove back to the lodge and, with the help of Mr. Smedley, packed up the rest of our belongings and a few pieces of furniture that had belonged to Dad's grandfather, which Mother wanted for the Denver house. This last was in effect a tacit admission of a change of some kind. Three of the four tires on the LaSalle had been blown out as the car tumbled down the rocks. Mr. Smedley took off the good wheel and tire but said nothing else was salvageable, given the inaccessible position of the wreck.

I was a student in Paris almost ten years later when the protracted negotiations with the Forest Service were finally completed and our section of river and boulders reentered the public realm as part of a plan for a string of small campgrounds at the Sluice Box and below. Old letters from Mother and Dad contain a few details about the slow collapse of the lodge—a heavy snowfall one winter, another boulder during a spring thaw. And word of the death of Mrs. Smedley. On a flight on a clear day from Seattle to Denver a few years back I was certain we flew over our section of the canyon but too high for me to make out any details. Friends urge me to look up the site on Google Earth. I prefer to remember it as it was.

An unexpected memory, one that is becoming more precise with time, is of the strange shape that demarked the main tunnels of the mine and the many smaller side tunnels, on sheets of almost-transparent paper that were regularly unrolled and spread out on the dining room table when the Slatters were visiting, corners held down by a crystal sugar bowl, a couple of porcelain dinner plates with worn gold edging, and rarely, when there was fresh fruit at Smedley's, a fruit bowl of the same design heaped with peaches and apricots and plums from the agricultural valley thirty miles beyond and a thousand feet below Basalt Junction. Penciled in more darkly, the main tunnels formed a shape like a stretched-out letter or character in an unfamiliar script, Cyrillic or Greek or even Japanese or Chinese, with spidery more lightly drawn secondary shafts leading off from them.

These drawings were for Mother, I think, images of doom that in fact were never to befall her or Dad. She was particularly fearful that on one of his frequent train trips up to the mine and back he would somehow trip and fall between the moving coaches and be cut in half—like his great-uncle two generations before, in Rockford, Illinois, who slipped on an icy platform. Dad lived into his nineties, as did Mother herself, despite in her case a string of illnesses and operations that tended to manifest themselves in the early days of summer, about the time we had been accustomed to pack the car for summer at the lodge.

I can't say how much they were aware of the mine's environmental despoliation, as we would call it today, and whether they ever thought through the connections between the tailing ponds, the dangerous tunnels, the mine deaths, and the comfortable life they led, a life that in turn bestowed on me a protected childhood and youth. Probably not. Indeed, why should they have? Their dwindling wealth was generated by the toxic processes of mining, but then so was the wealth of civilization as a whole: Miners die but no one stops using silver spoons to stir their coffee with, as Aunt Ruby once pointed out over dinner, while dropping lumps of sugar into her cup with little silver tongs. And, one can add, gold wedding bands remain in fashion, and diamonds continue to be sifted from the mud by the wretched of the earth.

They left those worries to Aunt Ruby, who as she grew older could not see misery in the streets or in the newspapers or on television without making the connections with her own well-being. They have so little and I have so much, she was fond of saying. The sharpness of her youth and middle age, when she was quick to uncover ulterior motives and hidden agendas, yielded in her old age to a diffuse sensitivity to the grand injustices of the world and the ghastly unfairness of it all. Though when it came to actual money she still insisted, *That* is to stay within the family. She approved of my profession but not who I worked for—Who would ever want to work for the government?—but even that was better than the way her son flitted through fads and enthusiasms on his meager trust fund, an irregular life I secretly envied.

Thus our days at the lodge, those sweet summers, came to an end. Without drama, other than that of a huge lump of volcanic rock, one among millions in the canyon, shifting position, as all had by fits and starts over the eons. And sooner or later as all would again and again, either one by one or in great rockslides or both, though with one miniscule difference: I would no longer be there to hear or see them.

It was years before I finally realized with a sharp pang that in the excitement of the last days I had left my ruby in its hiding place, in the knothole in the pine paneling, just above my upper bunk pillow. It might still be there, buried somewhere in the rubble.

There remain a few black-and-white photographs floating unglued within the black pages of an ornately scrolled album.

Dad, age two or so, lying on a bear rug somewhere outside in front of the lodge with his mother, my grandmother, facing the camera, with a short-haired black dog to one side, the three of them grouped around the bared jaws of the glass-eyed stuffed bear head, tattered fragments of which I discovered in a trunk in one of the spare rooms upstairs when I was six years old. Eventually I came to see the features of Grandmother Marianne, who died before I was born, echoed in Aunt Ruby—and even later, in my own visage.

Dad and Keith, Aunt Ruby's first husband, an Army Air Corps flyer who went down over the Philippines a couple of years before the beginning of the war, and three other men, family friends, all sprawled out in fishing hats and jackets and waders and holding their fly rods, on boulders somewhere near the lodge.

Mother, near the back porch, holding a dead rattlesnake by the tail, at arm's length, her head turned away.

Mother, same location and attitude except this time her eyes closed, holding a dead bobcat, its long spotted underbelly toward the camera.

The lodge, from a distance, with a half dozen open cars and sedans from the early 1930s parked at odd angles in front.

Dad, probably six, and Aunt Ruby, probably eight, holding the hands of their mother next to a passenger car, from whose open windows peer a half dozen male passengers, up at the tracks above the lodge.